THE TRAIN TO THE PLANE

HAIRBAG NATION

robert l. bryan

Published by robert l. bryan, 2023.

This is a work of fiction. Similarities to real people, places, or events are entirely coincidental.

THE TRAIN TO THE PLANE

First edition. July 22, 2023.

ISBN: 979-8223884019

Written by robert l. bryan.

For Meghan - the angel on my shoulder.

INTRODUCTION

Sticks and Stones is an English-language children's rhyme used as a defense against name-calling and verbal bullying, and is intended to increase resiliency, and avoid physical retaliation. The rhyme is reported to have first appeared in *The Christian Reporter* of March 1862, where it was presented as, *Sticks and stones may break my bones but words will never break me.* Versions that appeared in subsequent years evolved to *Sticks and stones may break my bones but names will never harm me.*

Just as the words changed slightly over time, so did the meaning. Initially, the speaker tries to develop the idea that sticks and stones may break bones, but words will leave no impact on him. He says that words are simply words; they don't have the power to hurt, tear, or tease someone's heart and soul. However, in the latter version of the poem, the speaker shifts the narrative and accepts the harmful impacts of unpleasant words and infers that words full of hatred chase the people like ghosts. The poet further highlights the impact of such words as piercing and sticking inside a person. Moreover, sticks and bats may crack bones, but sour words humiliate people. He adds that pain from words leaves a permanent scar on someone's mind and heart.

I believe this more recent interpretation of the rhyme is correct. Words do hurt and can be the cause of resorting to the sticks and stones. Try getting into an elevator with an overweight person and then proceed to read the elevator's weight capacity out load. Or perhaps try the more direct approach by telling a person their face makes onions cry or that they have so many gaps in their teeth it looks like their tongue is in jail. Maybe a more cerebral approach is the choice so you tell someone that if you wanted to kill yourself, you'd climb up that person's ego and jump down to their IQ. The point is that no matter how low or high-brow the insults, the words are likely to trigger a barrage of the aforementioned sticks and stones.

Insults can also be coded for use by personnel in certain groups. Every profession has its jargon or code words - but police slang can be particularly colorful. Whether the code words refer to vehicles, the actions of fellow officers, or the behavior of suspects, the slang is difficult for civilians to understand, which is the whole point of using the slang. Just as gang members use their tattoos as a sort of secret language, cops use slang to openly communicate with fellow officers without arousing suspicion from the public or those listening to chatter on police scanners. While some of the slang is relatively innocuous, other words and phrases are controversial and potentially offensive, and are reserved mainly for police locker rooms. One such slur that has been a staple of the police world – at least the police world in New York City – is the "Hairbag."

Hairbag is an archaic bit of slang with obscure origins. In police parlance, 'the bag' means 'the uniform.' Some officers believe "hairbag" is a riff on a longtime officer's uniform - so old it has become hairy. There are other theories to the term's origin, including cop's carrying a bag of hair to prove they were getting a haircut when they were off post. Regardless of the origin, being called a hairbag is not a complement. It usually refers to a veteran, burnt out cop who spends most of his patrol time avoiding work.

I don't know any cop who would want to be called a hairbag but it certainly isn't one of those hot, triggering words that would instantly result in a locker room brawl. That is why I was surprised and somewhat amused when I learned about a lawsuit filed a few years ago by a member of the NYPD. The suit alleged that the cop had suffered damage to his career because his boss had referred to him as a hairbag. The judge in the case eventually dismissed the suit, ruling that hairbag is a petty slight and not an example of any discrimination.

So, there you have it – an official ruling. The State of New York has decreed that hairbag isn't really a bad insult. Still, no cop wants to be considered a hairbag, and it is important to understand that hairbag is not a one size fits all term. There are different levels of hairbag skill.

A baseball player may possess great skills but only a select few possess the skills necessary to make it to the major leagues. And there are those major leaguers whose skills distinguish themselves from the other professional ballplayers. These elite athletes are inducted into the hall of fame. It is similar with hairbags. Some hairbags perform just the minimum effort required for many years of a lackluster, apathetic career. Then there is that rare breed of hairbag who stands out among the others and makes it into the hall of fame. Reaching the apex of hairbagdom sometimes requires good fortune. A hall of fame home run hitter may have been aided by playing his entire career in a stadium with a short right field fence. Similarly, a hairbag may have received a huge assist in reaching the hairbag hall of fame through assignment to a unit conducive to the traits of a hairbag. This is the story of one such unit. It is not a detective squad, narcotics or decoy unit. It is the tale of the cops assigned to the New York City Transit Police JFK Train to the Plane unit.

Back in the 1970s the New York City Transit Authority had a dream. Imagine if the subway system could provide a special train that would carry travelers from Midtown Manhattan to JFK Airport in an hour. Beginning in 1978 that dream became reality when New Yorkers could take the "Train to the Plane," an express subway train that ran down Avenue of the Americas in Manhattan and then made a nonstop dash to Kennedy International Airport. The train quickly became the crown jewel of the Transit Authority complete with specially installed luggage racks and a conductor who punched tickets. It even had a 10-second jingle that played on television as part of a promotional effort by the MTA.

The Train to the Plane got its start on Sept. 23, 1978, originating from the 57th Street station at Avenue of the Americas. The three-car train made stops at 47-50th Streets-Rockefeller Center, 42nd

Street-Bryant Park, 34th Street-Herald Square, West Fourth Street, Chambers Street at Church Street, Broadway-Nassau at Fulton Street, with an additional Brooklyn stop at Jay Street. Then — zoom! — straight to Howard Beach. Howard Beach? – that's not the airport. It turned out that the Train to the Plane was actually the train to the bus to the plane. The last stop was the Howard Beach station in Queens where shuttle buses, complete with luggage racks, waited to spirit passengers to their terminal. The fare for the train was $3.50 with trains running every twenty minutes from 6 a.m. to 2 a.m..

After a year, the train was handling about 2,000 rides a day, or 12 percent of all trips to J.F.K. from Manhattan. Gas shortages and two strikes on the city's bus lines helped attract interest — not to mention the infectious theme song, composed by Charles Morrow, a celebrated jingle writer and one-time collaborator with Simon & Garfunkel.

The train was not popular with a large segment of subway riders. The graffiti-free trains were the cleanest in the system, which some riders seemed to resent. These brand new air-conditioned J.F.K. trains pulled into stations with horns blaring and went gliding by almost always three-quarters empty, while thousands of commuters were resigned to stuff themselves into already overcrowded, hot and dirty trains.

The MTA was unconcerned about the negative public perception of the Train to the Plane. They had a clean, shiny, new train with a catchy television commercial and they were determined to keep the train's condition pristine. It didn't take a brain surgeon to figure out how to keep the Train to the Plane safe and clean – put a cop on each train. And so, the Train to the Plane Unit was born.

CHAPTER 1: The Train to the Plane

Frustrated - the word summed up the feelings of Sgt. Doug Collins during his past year with the New York City Transit Police. Approximately eighteen months earlier Doug's friend and former partner, Lt. Al Harlan, had reached out for Doug to supervise a new unit he was commanding. Doug became the supervisor of the Delta Squad, a small team within the newly formed Decoy Unit.

The Decoy Unit was formed to combat rising subway crime by employing undercover cops as decoys posing as various targets, such as businessmen out late after having a few drinks and tourists unfamiliar with the subway system. The Delta Squad was responsible for dealing with three specialized victim profiles. There had been an inordinate number of subway robberies against Asian high school students, Hasidic Jews, and cleaning women, so the undercovers in Doug's squad were selected to play the roles of these victim profiles.

After some initial growing pains, the Delta Squad was very successful, making several newsworthy arrests causing the spike of crimes against the aforementioned victim profiles to virtually disappear. The Delta Squad could not function indefinitely, especially when there were no significant crime statistics against the victim profiles the squad was suited to address. After six months in operation Lt. Harlan informed Doug that the Delta Squad was being disbanded. The squad members were given their choice of assignments, and they all chose to become part of a new unit Lt. Harlan was forming.

Robberies and other crimes were rampant in subway bathrooms, so Harlan was charged with putting together a squad to address the problem. Sgt. Collins and the other former members of Delta Squad got right to work in their new role, but before they could get going, politics intervened.

The subway bathrooms had long been an unofficial meeting place for men looking for anonymous sexual encounters. These men were also prime marks for subway criminals because many of these victims would be reluctant to report the crime for fear of their secret sexual encounters being revealed. The New York State Penal Law included the violation of loitering, and one of its subsections was loitering for the purpose of deviant sex. That section was used by transit cops for years to police the subway toilets. When a cop inspected a bathroom, and found men loitering inside, they were issued summonses for the aforementioned loitering section.

Three weeks after Doug's new squad went to work the New York State Supreme Court ruled that loitering for the purpose of deviant sex was unconstitutional. The knee jerk response of the City of New York, the Transit Authority, and the Transit Police Department was to immediately abandon any enforcement activities in subway bathrooms, including the new squad headed by Sgt. Collins. Once again, the squad members were given their choice of assignments. Doug Collins selected the Citywide Plainclothes Task Force. Doug did not fit the profile of many seventeen-year hairbags who were looking to ride out three years as easily as possible before retiring. Doug still had aspirations to make it into the Detective Division and he knew the only way this could be accomplished was assignment to the Task Force. There was just one small problem. The Task Force had two divisions - plainclothes and uniform. Doug had assumed he would be assigned to the plainclothes task force, and he was shocked when he received orders transferring him to the uniformed task force.

Al Harlan was empathetic to his friend's plight, but there was nothing he could do about it. To add insult to injury, Doug Collins was assigned to a specialized unit within the uniformed task force. Sgt. Collins was now a supervisor in the Train to the Plane Unit. A last-minute phone plea to George Reed, the huge, tough-talking Chief of Patrol, was Doug's last chance.

"Hello, Chief, it's Doug Collins."

"What do you want, Douglas," Reed huffed. "I'm very busy."

"Sorry to bother you, Chief, but when the unit handling the bathroom robberies was disbanded, I was told I was going to the plainclothes task force."

"So, what's the problem?" Reed asked.

"The problem is that I was assigned to the uniformed task force," Doug said.

"Are you kidding me?" the Chief bellowed. "You sound like a kid who didn't get what he wanted for Christmas."

"But, Chief, I was told…"

Reed cut Doug off in mid-sentence. "I don't care what you were told – deal with it. Besides," Reed continued, "the uniformed task force needs good sergeants like yourself."

"But Chief," Doug said, "I was assigned to The Train to the Plane."

"So?" Reed blurted.

"The Train to the Plane isn't a police unit," Doug said.

"What are you talking about?"

"The Train to the Plane Unit is a magnet for every hairbag on the job." Doug said. "It's hairbag heaven. Cops don't even have to try to be hairbags there. It's part of the job description."

"Poor you," the Chief moaned, his tone dripping with sarcasm. "Dougie didn't get what he wanted." Reed's voice transitioned to a snarl. "Wake up and join the rest of the world. Nobody gets what they want."

"This is the second time you're doing this to me," Doug said.

"What are you talking about?"

"I was already in the plainclothes task force and I got kicked out."

"How did you screw that up?" Reed chuckled.

"By trying to get the men to work," Doug replied. "The commanding officer said I was pressing the men too hard for summons and arrest activity so they sent me to the academy to supervise in-service training."

"A noble assignment," Reed snickered.

"Sure," Doug replied. "The instructors did a great job while I sat in an office reading the newspaper. It's like the department wanted me to become a hairbag."

"So, you have experience," Reed laughed. "It should be easy for you to become a hairbag again."

"Gee, thanks Chief. That makes me feel a lot better."

"Just do your job, Douglas." Reed growled as he slammed down the phone.

...

On Doug's first day assigned to the Train to the Plane Unit he was pleasantly surprised to find Sgt. Phil Kulesa waiting inside District 1 to provide him an orientation into the unit. Doug and Phil were both active cops when they worked together in District 3 ten years earlier. Doug considered Phil to be a straight shooter so as they leisurely strolled from Columbus Circle to the train's origination point at 57th Street, he knew he'd get the straight dope about the unit.

"There are sixty cops and ten sergeants assigned to the unit," Phil began, "and we all turn out of District 1."

"Sixty cops?" Doug blurted. "That's a lot, isn't it?"

"The trains run every twenty minutes from 6 a.m. to 2 a.m., seven days a week," Phil said. "Sixty cops barely covers the schedule."

"What do the cops do?" Doug asked.

"Not much," Phil chuckled. "They just ride the train and make sure no one gets on who shouldn't get on."

"How do they do that?"

"It's pretty simple," Phil explained. "The trains have three cars but only one door opens when the train makes a stop. The cop stands by the door and makes sure anyone trying to board is intending to take the Train to the Plane."

"Sounds complicated," Doug laughed.

"The assignment is a piece of cake," Phil replied. "Every hairbag in the city was scratching and clawing to get assigned to this unit."

"I never realized there were that many people going to the airport every day," Doug said.

Phil shook his head. "There's not. Half the people using the train go to the airport but the other half are residents of the Howard Beach area who are looking for a more civilized commute."

"What if there's a police condition on the platform when the train pulls in – what do they want the cop to do?" Doug asked.

"Nothing," Phil replied.

"Nothing?" Doug gasped.

Phil shrugged. "I guess I don't literally mean nothing. The cop should get on the radio and call it in, but if you're asking if the cop should get off his train to respond to a police condition on the platform – no!"

"Even if there is a guy laying on the platform with a knife sticking out of his chest," Doug remarked.

"The knife will still be in his chest when the first cop responding to the radio call gets there," Phil said. "Look," he continued. "As far as the MTA and Transit Police brass are concerned, the Train to the Plane is the pride of the subway fleet and they don't want anything pulling the cops off the trains."

"That philosophy is going to take some getting used to," Doug said.

"I know," Phil agreed. "It helps if you think of the cops as ships captains."

"What?"

"That's right," Phil nodded. "The cops are supposed to go down with their trains."

The two sergeants began descending the steps of the 57th Street station as Doug continued his questioning. "What do we do?"

"What do you mean?" Phil asked.

"What are the sergeants supposed to do?"

"Not much," Phil smiled. "We supervise cops who don't do too much, therefore, we don't do too much."

Doug shook his head. "This gets better and better."

"Look Dougie," Phil said, "I didn't create this unit, I just work in it. We do what every other sergeant on the job does – we supervise our cops. It's just a lot more one dimensional in our case."

"What's that mean?" Doug asked.

Phil swept his hand around the 57th Street station platform. "You either stand here at 57th Street and scratch the cop's memo books here or ride out to Howard Beach and scratch them there."

"Sounds complicated," Doug sighed.

"Hey," Phil shrugged. "That's the job."

"I know this may be a stupid question," Doug began, "but are there any activity quotas for the unit regarding summonses and arrests?"

Phil's face took on an incredulous look. "Are you kidding?" he said.

Doug held his hand up in a stop sign. "Forget I asked."

"This is an elite unit," Phil deadpanned. "We can't be bothered with activity quotas. That's why we are referred to as the Navy Seals of the Transit Police."

Doug ignored the comical response and pushed on. "Do the passengers have to have a ticket or do the conductors on the trains take cash?"

"Tickets for the Train to the Plane are sold at the booths," Phil said, "but the vast majority of the passengers pay the conductor on the train. That's one of the main reasons the cops are there – to watch over the money."

"Has any money ever been stolen from a conductor?" Doug asked.

"Not yet," Phil replied.

"If someone grabbed the money from the conductor," Doug asked, "would the cops be expected to abandon the train to chase the money?"

"Good question," Phil shrugged. "I guess we'll find out when it happens."

"Who is the commanding officer of our elite unit?" Doug asked.

"That's a complicated question," Phil said.

"How is it complicated?"

"Technically," Phil began, "we don't really have a commanding officer. The Train to the Plane unit is part of the uniformed task force so a task force lieutenant has been assigned, but he doesn't really hold the title of commanding officer."

"Okay," Doug said, "that's not complicated."

"It is when the lieutenant is Clifford Beasley," Phil responded.

"Sergeant Beasley from District 3?" Doug gasped.

"The one and only," Phil nodded. "Do you remember him?"

"He was an asshole!" Doug blurted.

Phil smiled. "Then you'll be happy to know our fearless leader hasn't changed as a lieutenant. Even though he is not really a commanding officer he signs all his department correspondence as 'commanding officer' and he even had business cards made that refers to him as 'commanding officer.'"

"Well," Doug sighed, "with a unit like this that has nothing much to do, how bad can it be, even with a boss like Beasley?"

Phil laughed. "You'll see."

CHAPTER 2: The Assignment

A year in the Train to the Plane unit gave Doug Collins ample opportunity to get a good feel for how it would be under the command of Lt. Clifford Beasley – and it wasn't good. It seemed like a case of déjà vu for Doug. Once a motivated sergeant in the plainclothes task force, he had been unceremoniously dumped into the Police Academy to read the newspaper all day while his staff of instructors conducted in-service training classes. After getting his police juices flowing again in the Decoy Unit's Delta Squad, instead of returning to the plainclothes task force, as he had requested, Doug was sent to the hairbag-infested Train to the Plane Unit within the uniformed task force. He spent the last twelve months aimlessly wandering the 57th Street and Howard Beach stations, meeting arriving trains to sign the memo books of the assigned cops.

There was a big difference between his time at the academy and his present assignment. The lieutenant at the police academy realized there was not much for the in-service training sergeant to do and basically left Doug alone to sit in the office and read the paper. Clifford Beasley, however, did not share similar sentiments regarding his Train to the Plane Unit and the sergeants assigned to the unit.

From the time he first encountered him in District 3, Doug pegged Beasley as the classic case of a Napoleonic complex. He barely passed the police height requirement in place at the time, and he was a very soft and flabby 150-pounds. As a sergeant in District 3 Beasley seemed to relish breaking the cops balls for everything from shoes that weren't shined to his reinstruction for moustaches that were just slightly longer than the department manual allowed. Now, over ten years later, Doug noted that Beasley's hunched posture made him look even shorter than he remembered, and he was still soft and flabby, but now his frame carried at least 175-pounds.

Doug's mouth hung open in disbelief during much of his first meeting with Lt. Beasley. Beasley explained with great pride how the Train to the Plane was the jewel of the Transit Authority and that the Train to the Plane Unit was the most elite unit in the Transit Police Department. Doug nearly choked on his coffee when he heard that claim, and even though intelligence and common sense told him not to respond to the boast, he just couldn't help himself.

"Excuse me, lieutenant," Doug said, "did I just hear you correctly?"

"What do you mean?"

"Did you say that the Train to the Plane is the most elite unit in the Transit Police Department?"

"That's right, sergeant," Beasley scowled. "Do you have a problem with that?"

Doug shrugged. "Well, sir, I looked at the unit roster and I would say you do have some elite hairbags assigned."

Doug Collins likely never would have had a good working relationship with Lt. Clifford Beasley, but that brief exchange sealed the deal. From that moment on, any assignment Beasley felt Doug would not like fell into his lap. Doug was content to wander between 57th Street and Howard Beach, but at least half the time Beasley kept Doug squirreled away inside the Train to the Plane's little office inside District 1 working on every administrative and statistical report he could think up.

Doug's usual strategy when beginning his tour of duty was to try to get into uniform and depart District 1 before having any interaction with Lt. Beasley. There was a serious flaw in that plan, however, because Doug had to walk past the Train to the Plane office to leave the district. It had become an involuntary action for him to hold his breath as he walked those last thirty feet toward the district door, hoping he would not hear the whiney voice shouting "Collins, get over here!"

One morning about a year into his tenure with the unit, Doug had not yet fully inhaled when the call summoned him into the Train to the Plane office. Lt. Beasley sat at his desk with a look of pure contentment on his face. Part of the contentment had to do with the brilliant idea he had, but the other aspect that brought him great joy was the pained look on Doug's face at having to perform another one of his assignments.

"I have a little job for you to do," Beasley said.

"Yes, sir," Doug sighed.

"This is an important one, so don't screw it up," Beasley warned.

"Aren't all your jobs important, Lieutenant?"

Beasley pointed his index finger at Doug. "Don't be a smartass!"

Doug threw his hands up," Sorry, no offense meant," he remarked insincerely.

Beasley cleared his throat. "It's about time this unit got the recognition it deserves."

"I totally agree," Doug smirked. "How do we do that?"

Beasley's chest puffed with pride. "By winning the unit citation."

Doug recoiled in horror. "Excuse me, Lieutenant, are we talking about the same unit citation – the one the department awards each year to the most outstanding unit in the Transit Police Department."

"That's the only unit citation I know of," Beasley glared. "And you will write the report that will get us that award."

"Hold on," Dog stammered. "What am I supposed to write in this report? – how many hours our cops stood on the train without sitting down or falling asleep."

"You're trying my patience, Collins," Beasley warned. He pointed to the row of black binders in the bookshelf next to his desk. "In those binders you'll find all the documentation you need to make the case that our unit was the most outstanding in the department. Now get to work!"

"Yes, sir," Doug said as he began to make his exit from the office.

"Collins!" Beasley bellowed, forcing Doug to stick his head back in the office doorway. "Just remember, if I don't get this unit citation it will be your ass."

"Of course, Lieutenant," Doug smiled, "and my ass would deserve it."

It took Doug less than an hour to go through all the binders. During the year the members of the unit had handled eighteen aided cases where passengers had gotten sick on the train and three of the cops had received attaboy letters from the chief resulting from passengers writing to the chief to tell them what a great job the cops had done – great police work like explaining to them the easiest way to get from Heathrow to Piccadilly Circus, and what were the best attractions to see at Disney World. That was it! Doug was supposed to chronicle those heroic acts and convince a committee of chiefs to bestow the unit citation on the Train to the Plane Unit.

Doug slammed the last binder closed, leaned back in his chair and stretched. He rotated his head slowly in an attempt to release the tightness that had built in his neck. During one rotation to the left his head stopped abruptly. On a shelf in the far corner of the room sat another binder. This binder sat alone, far away from the ones Beasley had directed Doug to use. Doug rose from the chair and moved toward the binder, squinting to read the label on the spine as he approached. "Incidents," he mouthed as he grabbed the binder and returned to the desk.

As Doug began paging through the binder a smile appeared on his face and it grew wider and wider with each page he turned. He bit his lip and nodded as he grabbed a sheet of memo paper and inserted it into the typewriter. With his two index fingers he pecked the subject "Justification for Unit Citation Award." He moved down two spaces and began at the left margin "Justification 1." Doug quickly paged back through the binder until he found the page he was looking for and continued with the first justification, "Police Officer Donald Campos."

Doug sat back, rubbed his hands together and took a deep breath. If Lt. Beasley wanted a report requesting the unit citation for the Train to the Plane unit, that's exactly what he would get, and it would be a report he would never forget.

CHAPTER 3: The Story of Police Officer Donald Campos

"Lt. Beasley, phone call for you on line two."

Clifford Beasley did not hide his annoyance at being disturbed by the message from the District 1 assistant desk officer. His latest project was attempting to get the department to authorize a unit patch for the Train to the Plane Unit, and he was in the middle of sketching what he believed would be a patch design the entire department would be envious of.

Beasley slammed down his pencil and picked up the phone. "Lt. Beasley."

"Good morning, Lieutenant, this is Captain Tom Dominguez with the Tampa International Airport Police."

"What can I do for you, Captain?" Beasley asked.

"This is something of an odd situation," Captain Dominguez snickered, "but do you have a Police Officer Campos working in your unit?"

"Yes, Donald Campos," Beasley replied.

"Is Campos working today?" The Captain inquired.

"Yes, he's working 6 a.m. to 2 p.m.," Beasley said. "Is something wrong? Did something happen to a family member of his down there?"

"No, no, nothing like that," Captain Dominguez assured. "But do you know where he is right now?"

"Just a moment," Beasley grabbed the daily roll call sheet and quickly scanned through it. "He's on his meal period right now at the Howard Beach station."

"Well, that's interesting," Dominguez chuckled.

"Why is that interesting?" Beasley asked.

"Because New York City Transit Police Officer Donald Campos is sitting across from me in full uniform in my office in Tampa International Airport."

•••

When a person is identified in the media with his middle name included, it is usually a story about a serial killer. The news story might indicate that "Billy Bob Watson" maintained his innocence regarding the six murders or "Jimmy Ray Dooley" showed no remorse during his sentencing for the killings. Police Officer Campos was not a murderer or criminal of any kind, yet, he was routinely referred to by his colleagues as "Don Juan Campos." To confuse the issue further, Juan was not his middle name. The name on his birth certificate was DONALD RICHARD CAMPOS. Legalities mattered little to his friends on the Transit Police Department. To everyone working on the Train to the Plane Unit, he was Don Juan Campos.

Don Campos was proud of his moniker and he had worked tirelessly to achieve it. Don loved women - all shapes, sizes, races, and ethnicities. He truly was an equal opportunity lover. Several years before NBA legend Wilt Chamberlain published his biography in which he claimed to have slept with twenty thousand women in his lifetime, Don Juan Campos was making a similar boast regarding his eighteen years with the New York City Transit Police. Don did not place a specific number on his conquests, but he asserted that during his career his female conquests numbered in the thousands.

Don was well suited for his female obsession. At forty-one years of age he was tall and lean and still possessed boyish good looks that females seemed to find irresistible. The girls seldom pointed to one feature that made Don so handsome, though they all seemed to love his eyes which generated an intensity, honesty, and gentleness - qualities they would ultimately discover were a facade. Don's years on uniformed patrol had accustomed him to women stopping in their tracks at the sight of him. He recognized the sudden pause in their natural expression followed by overcompensating with a nonchalant gaze and a weak smile followed by the inevitable blush.

Don did his best to accommodate the desires of all his female fans. Besides allotting all his off-duty time to the ladies he also conducted many liaisons while on duty. The stories were legendary including sex in porter's rooms, signal rooms, and in the conductor's cab of a moving train. One of Don's more classic encounters occurred on a midnight shift when he was working in District 12 in the Bronx. Don was patrolling an elevated station on a hot summer night when a female ending a night at a local bar made her way up to the station to take the subway home. Overnight trains run every twenty minutes, but it took Don less than five minutes to persuade the tipsy young lady to partake in some fun with him. The only problem was that this station had no room to use for the session, not even a bathroom. The lack of a room was no obstacle to Don. He escorted his guest up to the deserted platform and led her to the dark back end. There, she quickly dropped to her knees and went to work. Don was in a state of total bliss and did not react to the light of the train coming around the bend, nor did he hear the accompany rumbling. The motorman nearly overshot the station when his train light lit up the performance on the platform like the spotlight of a Broadway show. The woman's head movement increased in speed as the door of the train opened. The rear car was empty except for a young cop performing train patrol. The cop stuck his head out the door and stared at the action on the platform like a deer caught in the glare of headlights.

"She lost a contact lens," Don gasped. "I'm helping her look for it."

The young cop stared at the gurgling woman and said, "Good luck, I hope she finds it," just before the doors closed.

A life of conquests was not without casualties. Don had been through four marriages and swore that he would never walk down the aisle again – a promise he had made after signing each divorce settlement. Additionally, his career with the Transit Police had been mediocre at best. He made very few arrests and didn't write many summonses. He only generated enough activity to keep the bosses off his back so he could focus on his ladies. His discipline and sick record were also spotty. Don had been on the chronic sick list several times because he had called out sick on occasions when he just had to meet some special ladies. Don had also been written up a few times when he was caught off his post. The reason he was off post was always the same. He had been in pursuit of a female and just could not bear the thought of letting her get away.

Don claimed to have a little Native American blood in him and he regularly became philosophical when speaking about his obsession with women. "When a brave has become his good wolf self, as the Cherokee legend tells, he is handsome to every female eye and heart." That quote alone was almost enough to get him christened with the nickname of Chief Rising Hardwood, but once again, the Native Americans lost out and Don Juan Campos won the day.

The Train to the Plane Unit was a Godsend for Don Juan Campos. Not only could he ride out the last few years of his career without having to generate any summons or arrest activity, but it opened up a whole new category of female to him. It wasn't just residents of Howard Beach and airline passengers who rode the train to the plane, it was also airline employees who used the service. Don was only interested in one type of airline employee who rode the Train to the Plane - the stewardess. After a year in the unit Don's trophy case contained flight attendants from almost every airline that flew out of JFK.

Lisa Andrews, however, was the one trophy that had eluded him, and the more he kept striking out with her the more he desperately wanted her. Don had become completely infatuated with the American Airlines flight attendant. She had a beauty that made those billboard-princesses look paper thin. Don loved her curves and softness. With the muscles of an athlete and the blessed fat of a baby, Lisa was the most astonishing woman Don had ever met – easy to talk to and fun to be with during the hour ride from Manhattan to Howard Beach. Her beauty was complete, but Don found it difficult to describe – it was just there. Lisa was working a hop from JFK to Tampa and Don would see her on the train three times a week when she traveled from her Manhattan hotel to the airport. He had tried every approach and line but although she was very sociable, Don was unable to get Lisa to agree to a date.

There was something different about Don's first train on that Tuesday morning. Lisa Andrews was on the train, looking as beautiful and desirable as ever, but there was something different about her. Maybe it was her smile or the twinkle in her eyes, but there was something that communicated to Don that he may be breaking through her barrier.

Don went to work immediately and as the Train to the Plane sailed through Brooklyn he had progressed to the point where Lisa mentioned that she had heard wonderful things about Angelina's, an Italian restaurant on Bleecker Street, but that she had never eaten there. Don initiated a full court press and by the time the train pulled into Howard Beach he had offered to take Lisa to Angelina's on any day of the week at any time of the day or night. As she departed the Howard Beach station to board the shuttle bus to the airport, Lisa said she would think about Don's offer.

This fish that had gotten away so many times was sniffing around the bait, so Don had no intention of pulling his line out of the water. He followed Lisa onto the shuttle bus and plopped down in the seat beside her. All the way to the airport he continued pressing for the date at Angelina's. When the bus pulled to a stop at the American Airlines departures gate he had resorted to outright begging and pleading for the date. All through the terminal and up to the gate Lisa was barraged with "please" "I beg you" "why not" "Just once" and "trust me." Lisa seemed amused by the pathetic display and no one was going to stop a police officer in uniform, not even when that police officer followed his prey down the jetway and onto the aircraft.

•••

Clifford Beasley wanted to make sure he had received the message correctly. "Could you repeat that please, Captain."

"Sure," Dominguez replied. "Police Officer Donald Campos is sitting in front of my desk right now."

"And you are in Tampa," Beasley continued.

"That's right," Dominguez confirmed.

"In Florida," Beasley said.

"The only Tampa I know of is in Florida," Dominguez chuckled.

"May I have a word with Officer Campos?" Beasley asked.

"Of course," Dominguez said.

"Hello. Lieutenant," Don sighed.

"What the hell is going on, Officer?" Beasley roared.

"Keep calm, Lieutenant," Don said, "this is really not a big deal."

"Not a big deal?" Beasley's voice rose two octaves. "You're on duty right now and you are in Florida. This is a very big deal. Now what the hell happened?"

"It's kind of a long story," Don began, "but I was ready to jump on a flight back to New York and I would have been back to go off duty at the end of my tour if the airport police hadn't stopped me."

"Put the Captain back on the phone," Beasley snapped.

"What would you like me to do, Lieutenant?" Dominguez asked.

"Would it be possible to put him on a flight to New York?" Beasley asked.

"Sure, He'll be on his way back to you in twenty minutes," Dominguez said. "I just wanted to make sure you knew he was here."

"Thank you very much, Captain," Beasley said. "You can rest assured that I will be at the airport to meet him."

Beasley did meet Don at the airport and immediately suspended him from duty pending formal disciplinary charges. A week later Don had the last laugh when his union attorney successfully argued that Don was guilty of nothing more than extending his meal period without authorization. His penalty was a three-day suspension without pay which he had already served prior to the hearing.

Whenever a fellow cop would ask if his trip to Tampa was worth the three-day loss of pay, Don would smile, wink and remark, "Sometimes it costs time and money to land that big fish that always gets away, but when it finally takes your bait and you reel it in, the money it cost is secondary to the feeling of conquest."

CHAPTER 4: The Story of Police Officer George Lutz

Doug continued paging through the thick binder. The unit citation would need a lot more than a flight to Florida. Lt. Beasley would expect him to write a compelling argument for the award, and that was what he intended to do. Doug stopped flipping the pages and squinted as he focused on the subject line of the incident - BOOTH ROBBERY ARREST. Doug was perplexed. The robbery of a subway token booth was a big deal, and an arrest for a booth robbery is something that any unit would laud in a report requesting the unit citation. He wondered why he had never heard about this arrest and why the details of the event were contained within the incident folder. Three pages later, everything would be clear.

...

George Lutz was not looking for much out of life. The seventeen-year veteran was an original member of the Train to the Plane Unit, and he was a perfect fit for the squad. George wasn't much of a cop, nor did he ever want to be. He wanted a job that offered the salary and benefits to afford him a middle-class existence and the Transit Police fit the bill. Before the Train to the Plane came along George had bounced around between District 4 in Manhattan and Districts 30 and 33 in Brooklyn. In each assignment George was never a problem for his bosses, but he always provided just the minimum amount of effort and activity to stay under their radar.

When George joined the Train to the Plane Unit he was in search of one thing, and it had nothing to do with police work. George Lutz was looking for love. He was not one of the snakes in a blue uniform trolling the subway for anything resembling a female. George was sincerely looking for a woman to love. George Lutz was twenty-one when he became a transit cop. Two years later he married his childhood sweetheart Karen Kingsley. Karen could not have children but George was content going through life with just his soulmate by his side. Five years ago, George returned from work one early evening to find Karen complaining of a headache. It seemed like nothing more than the job for a couple of aspirins, but two weeks later George held his wife's hand as she passed away in a hospital bed from a brain tumor.

George was stunned. It was as if a piece of himself had been cut out of his body. Two years passed without George having any thoughts about entering into a relationship with another woman. The pain from his loss seemed to increase with the passage of time. His sister urged George to begin socializing again, explaining that it would be the only way to deal with his depression.

George reluctantly accepted his sister's advice, but he was less than enthusiastic in his search for female companionship. He attended numerous events for divorced and widowed singles but he always ended the evenings alone. He even accompanied one of the other cops from the unit to a bar in Queens that the cop characterized as crawling with hot women. George had to admit that the bar was crawling with women, but most of them appeared to be approaching seventy years of age. When George pointed out the advanced age of the crowd, the cop shrugged and said, "Why do you think they call this place the last chance saloon."

It can be amazing how something you are seeking could be right in front of you but you don't see it. George liked having set routines, and the Train to the Plane Unit was perfect for him. George worked steady 6 a.m. to 2 p.m.. Every day his meal hour was always at Howard Beach after his third train run. There was no exact time the train would pull into the Howard Beach station, but it was sometime around 11 a.m.. The Train to the Plane had to keep a tighter schedule than most subway trains because most of the passengers had flights to catch.

When the train arrived at Howard Beach George would wait until all the passengers detrained, then he would walk upstairs to the token booth. Unit cops were required to call the Citywide Task Force headquarters to report on and off meal, so the first stop for George was always the token booth where he would ask the booth clerk to release the latch on the compartment on the side of the booth that would allow him access to the booth phone. On most days it would be Rita McNeil providing the phone access to George.

Rita was a pretty lady about the same age as George, and like George, she was a widow. Aside from the morning rush hour, Howard Beach was not a particularly busy station and George enjoyed the opportunity to stand outside the booth engaging Rita in conversation. It reached a point where he would rarely go anywhere for his hour meal period, but would instead stand outside the booth talking to Rita. Booth clerks weren't supposed to allow anyone entry into the token booth. Even police officers were not permitted inside the booth unless there was a police emergency occurring. It didn't take long, however, for Rita to break that rule. It was the first day of a sub-freezing temperature with George shivering outside the booth that she turned the latch on the door and allowed him in. That action of unlocking the booth door was symbolic, as she was also unlocking the door to her heart. It was at that moment that George and Rita became a couple.

George and Rita's relationship blossomed quickly, and they talked about marriage, but both were reluctant. They weren't sure if there would be any impact on their assignments if a Train to the Plane cop was married the token booth clerk at Howard Beach, one of the terminal points for the Train to the Plane. Neither wanted to risk being transferred, so for the time being they kept their relationship very quiet.

Rita had a ten-year-old daughter attending Catholic School in Howard Beach. Most of the students in the school went home for lunch with a small section of the auditorium set aside for those students who did not have a parent home during lunch time. Rita's daughter hated staying at school for lunch while all her friends went home, but there was nothing she could do about it - until George came up with an idea.

Rita lived only ten minutes away from the Howard Beach station, but her one-hour lunch break did not give her time to pick up her daughter at school, bring her home for lunch, and bring her back to school. She would need about two hours. George decided to use his routine to his and Rita's advantage. When George detrained for his lunch period there was usually a sergeant waiting on the platform to give him a scratch. After signing his memo book, the sergeant would board the train returning to Manhattan, leaving George to proceed with his meal period. A cop's meal period was an hour long, but George's next assigned train was not for two hours. Technically, when George called off meal he was supposed to patrol the Howard Beach station for an hour, but in reality, after calling off meal he just continued with another hour break until he had to board his assigned train.

It was George who suggested that he would cover for Rita in the token booth while she was bringing her daughter home for lunch. Rita was reluctant at first, but the more George pressed her the more the idea sounded attractive to her, especially when Phyllis Brown agreed to play along. Phyllis Brown was the booth clerk assigned to perform meal reliefs in the area including the Howard Beach Station. Every day sometime around noon Phyllis would take over the booth while Rita went to lunch. Phyllis agreed to the plan when George explained that she would get an extra hour break for herself by not having to relieve Rita at the Howard Beach Booth. All that remained now was to deal with how George looked. With all the time he spent inside the booth with Rita he was sure he could perform the job of selling tokens, and the booth at Howard Beach never got busy in the middle of the day. The potential problem lay in the fact that a uniformed police officer would be inside the booth selling token, and would likely result in some member of the public reporting the strange sight.

A recent change in New York City Transit policy provided the answer to George's dilemma. For most of the existence of subway token booths and the clerks manning them, the dress regulations for the clerks was casual at best. But about two years earlier the Transit Authority made a 180-degree about face. Booth clerks were now required to wear a bright red sports jacket with the TA logo on the left breast, a white dress shirt, dark blue tie, black dress pants and black shoes. George could assemble the entire wardrobe easily except for the bright red sports coat. For that he would need the assistance of a friend in the Transit Authority. The friend worked in the TA stockroom in Long Island City, and it took one brief visit to the stockroom for George to emerge with his own official bright red booth clerk sport coat.

A new routine was soon added to George's repertoire. When his train arrived at Howard Beach he expressed an odd reaction for a cop who spied a sergeant waiting on the platform for him - he was gleeful. The sergeant would sign his memo book and initiate some mindless small talk until boarding the train for the trip back to Manhattan. The departing train was George's cue to dash up to the mezzanine where Rita would open the token booth door and hand him a shopping bag he kept stashed inside the booth. After a quick stop in an employee bathroom George returned to the booth decked out in his bright red sports coat and white shirt. George had made the decision that he only needed the white shirt and red sport coat to play his role. He kept his uniform pants and shoes on, and he used his police tie. He also wore his gun belt when he realized that the red jacket hid its presence, especially when he was inside the token booth.

After a quick kiss Rita was flying up the stairs on her way to pick up her daughter. George tuned the radio to his favorite country music station and settled into the uncomfortable stool, ready to sell some tokens. An hour later George tapped a rhythm to the music with his fingers on the counter. He was bored. He had sold three tokens and was looking for something to do to pass the time. He looked to the left and noticed a clipboard hanging on the booth wall. It was the token reconciliation sheet and it showed that the wheels hadn't been pulled since Rita's shift began.

At various times of the day and night token clerks were required to leave the booth and go to the turnstiles to remove the tokens from the turnstiles and bring them back into the booth to be sold again. They recorded the retrieval of the tokens on the token reconciliation sheet. The retrieval of the tokens was always a sensitive time because "pulling the wheels" as it was known in transit jargon made the clerk vulnerable because they were alone, outside the booth. George routinely urged Rita not to pull her wheels unless a cop was on the station, and he welcomed the opportunity to pull the wheels for her while she was serving lunch to her daughter.

George grabbed the clipboard and the keyring hanging next to it. He picked up the bucket on the floor and pushed open the door. George approached the array of four turnstiles and dropped the bucket onto the concrete floor. He placed the clipboard on top of the turnstile and leaned his head in very close to read the number displayed on the small meter on the turnstile. He recorded the number on the sheet and then used the key to open a small door on the bottom of the turnstile. George opened the door and removed a metal container seated in the bottom of the turnstile. He carefully turned the container, pouring a load of tokens into the bucket. He placed the empty container back into the turnstile, closed and locked the door and moved with the clipboard and bucket onto the next turnstile.

George always preached situational awareness to Rita, and how she should always be aware of everything going on around her, especially when she was pulling her wheels. But now, George was so focused on his task at the turnstiles he failed to practice what he preached. He never saw the dark figure standing behind a column in the corner of the mezzanine. He didn't notice the figure moving towards him. He didn't see the figure reach into his pocket and emerge holding a gun. The first notice George had of the figure was when the male voice snarled "Do exactly what I say or I'll blow your head off."

It was unclear who was more shocked - George at being accosted by an armed robber from behind or the crook after his victim spun around revealing a Transit Authority token booth clerk wearing a full gun belt. For a long instant the two adversaries stood frozen, staring into each other's eyes, attempting to access the scene in front of them. George was the first to move and less than a minute later the perpetrator was face down on the concrete with his hands cuffed behind his back.

Armed robberies of any kind in the subway were big deals, but a booth holdup was special in the world of transit policing. George had not even begun celebrating his trophy arrest when the multitude of sirens gaining in volume told him he had a problem. The first thought entering George's head after his prisoner was secure was for him to take off his red jacket and white shirt and then radio for assistance and make it look like he had walked up upon the booth hold up. With any luck he would be able to hold off on making the radio call for a few more minutes until Rita returned to the booth. Those sirens, however, indicated that the plan was not viable. A concerned member of the public had come down the stairs and walked into the scene of the perpetrator holding a gun on the red jacketed booth clerk. The frightened man had made a quick about face, scurrying up the stairs to the first payphone he spied on the street. In a matter of seconds, they all would be on the station - transit cops, city cops, sergeants and duty captains - all trying to figure out why the cop was wearing a booth clerk's outfit. As an added bonus Lt. Beasley had been attending a community board meeting in Queens and had responded to Howard Beach when he heard the radio call.

All matter of schemes and scams ran through George's head, but in the end, he fell on his sword and fessed up to the truth. Lt. Beasley was doubly outraged. His Train to the Plane unit usually generated no enforcement activity, and now he had a cop who interrupted a booth holdup and arrested the perpetrator - real police work. But how could the lieutenant boast of the achievement when his officer took the action while impersonating a booth clerk who had abandoned her post. Beasley just couldn't fathom not receiving proper credit for the arrest so he tried to convince the Chief of Patrol that he planned the whole charade. He said he utilized his own initiative to institute "Operation Red Jacket," and that George had been on the station dressed as a booth clerk at his direction.

The Chief of Patrol, George Reed, was a large, gruff man who never minced words. When the Chief learned about Operation Red Jacket he called Beasley and explained that if he heard about Operation Red Jacket again, it would become Operation Red Nose because that's what color Beasley's nose would be after he landed a punch square on it.

As for George, he escaped discipline because Lt. Beasley couldn't write him up after trying to claim that he had organized the operation. Less than a year later George and Rita were married, and in a case of ironic transit police humor, at the wedding George and his ushers were all dressed in red jackets with the Transit Authority logo on the left breast.

The Operation Red Jacket arrest melted into the obscurity of an incident binder, never to be resurrected again. That is, until Doug Collins decided the incident would be perfect to cite as a reason the Train to the Plane Unit should be awarded the unit citation.

CHAPTER 5: The Story of Police Officer Leo Fromme

Leo Fromme wanted desperately to make it big in the business world. The only problem was that he was a transit cop with the boldest moves he ever made being deciding to call in sick when he wasn't really ill.

For most of his sixteen years on the job, the Transit Police Department was an afterthought to Leo. He spent the overwhelming majority of his time initiating a series of failed entrepreneurial endeavors he hoped would skyrocket him out of the subway and into the world of high finance. Unfortunately for Leo, his idea of trying to make it big in the business world involved falling for just about every work at home scam in existence. Leo tried them all. He lost money on a stuffing envelopes opportunity that was supposed to supply a steady second income. He also jumped at the opportunity to pay a small registration fee so that he could make $250 a week carving cupid arrows out of wood blocks. Leo sat in his garage for weeks carving arrows only to have every arrow rejected by the company as being flawed and not carved according to the supplied instructions. The only thing stopping Leo from being scammed out of big money was the fact that he didn't have much money to give away. He was stuck losing fifty to a hundred dollars at a time on these scams.

When a distant uncle who Leo could not remember ever meeting passed away and left him eight thousand dollars, the money was just burning a hole in his pocket. He wanted to strike out into the business world once more, but he had learned his lesson with the work at home scams.

Leo saw the ad in the newspaper and his heart began beating faster with excitement. The opportunity to own his own vending machines was staring him in the face. Vending machines weren't a scam. He knew a guy who hung out in the neighborhood bar whose full-time job was owning vending machines. Of course, Leo wasn't considering that his bar buddy had eighty machines spread out at locations all over the city, while the ad offered two machines – one soda and one candy machine for eight thousand dollars. And the best part was that the company supplying the machines would find a location and would maintain them if they required repairs.

Leo couldn't restrain himself. Within a week he was sitting in the nondescript office of C&C Vending, signing the contract that made him the proud owner of two vending machines. Leo was like a kid impatiently waiting for Christmas to arrive. Santa finally crawled down the chimney in the form of a call from C&C Vending informing Leo that his machines were being placed in the waiting room a new car dealership only two miles from his home. The vending company representative told Leo it was an exceptional location because not only would his machines receive business from people waiting for their cars to be serviced, but they would also be frequented by the dealership employees.

Leo ran out to a local wholesaler and bought a huge supply of candy, snacks and soda. The more he bought, the lower his price per unit and the larger his profit would be for each item sold from his machines. Leo was like a proud father when he finished filling the machines for the first time. He took a couple of steps back, smiled and took a deep breath as he thought about laying in his bath tub covered in all the quarters the machines would bring in.

Leo planned to make weekly visits to the dealership to restock the machines and pick up his booty of coins. Two days after he had filled the machines, however, he couldn't restrain himself. When Leo stepped inside the waiting room there was an explosion in his brain... the good sort... the type that carries more possibilities than he could be conscious of. The machines were empty. They had sold out in two days. Hundreds of ideas of the riches he would reap raced through his head like electricity... he could feel it. His hand was shaking as he attempted to put the key into the candy machine. Finally, the key fit into the lock and Leo quickly turned it to the right. He opened the small burlap bag he had brought with him just in case the overflowing coins spilled out when he opened the door. Leo pulled back the door and pressed the bag up against the opening. There was silence. Not one coin spilled out of the door. Leo took a deep breath. There wasn't any problem. The coin box was probably large enough to accommodate all the coins from a fully stocked machine. Leo reached through the door and yanked out the metal coin box. Leo's brain stuttered for a moment as every part of him went on pause while his thoughts caught up. Almost robotically his hands rose to rub his eyes, hoping he may wipe away the reality. The coin box was empty. With a sense of doom, he quickly switched keys and opened the empty soda machine – empty coin box.

Leo stepped back until he slowly slumped into a chair – a defeated man. He stared at those empty machines for five full minutes without making a move. A young salesman dressed in a shirt and tie entered the waiting room jiggling some quarters in his hand, but stopped short when he saw the empty machines. He glanced at Leo and smiled. "Too late, the boys already got to them."

The comment snapped Leo out of his trance. "What?"

"The vending machines," the salesman explained. "I heard new ones were put in a couple of days ago and I wanted to get to them before the boys did – but I see I'm too late." The salesman shook his head. "When will these vending people learn?"

Leo shot out of the chair. "What are you talking about? What boys?"

"The boys working in the service department. With these older type machines, they figured out how to activate them without putting any coins in by sliding a wire into the coin slot."

"They all do it?" Leo gasped.

"Only a couple of them are really good at it," the salesman replied, "but that doesn't matter. The experts get everything out of the machines for the rest of the staff."

"What happens after that?" Leo asked.

"Nothing," the salesman shrugged. "It's just a matter of how long the owner of the machine keeps filling them up before he gives up and gets rid of them. I think the most has been four times." The salesman tapped the window of the empty candy machine. "It's like Christmas here when new vending machines come in. Now we just have to see how stupid the owner of the machine is, and how many times he refills them."

"Yeah," Leo groaned. "The guy must have been very stupid to get into the business in the first place."

"Oh well," the salesman said, "I guess I have to go across the street for my soda."

Leo's next stop was the pay phone on the wall of the waiting room.

"Hello, C&C Vending – can I help you?"

"This is Leo Fromme. I recently bought two machines from you."

"Oh yes, how's it going, Mr. Fromme?"

"Not very good."

"Oh no, what seems to be the problem?"

"Evidently, the machines you sold me can be easily operated by sliding a wire through the coin slot. I visited the machines just now and found all the candy and soda gone and not one coin in either machine."

"That's terrible. Did you file a police report?"

"That's not gonna do any good. I need servicing on the machines immediately so that slipping in a wire won't activate them."

"That would not be maintenance, Mr. Fromme. That would be an upgrade."

"How much would this upgrade cost me?"

"Hmm...ballpark figure I would say about four thousand dollars for both machines."

"Four thousand dollars? You're out of you mind. Look, I don't want the machines. It says in my contract that I have thirty days to return them, so I am returning them for a refund."

"That's your choice, Mr. Fromme. As soon as you return the keys to the machines our office we'll cut you a check for four thousand dollars."

"Four thousand? You mean eight thousand, don't you?"

"Your contract entitles you to a refund of fifty percent of the purchase price. It's right there in your contract. The check will be here for you whenever you decide to drop off the keys. Have a good day. Mr. Fromme."

Leo Fromme's business ventures had reached a new low. Not only was he out four thousand dollars, but he had a garage filled with soda, candy and snacks that would take his family a year to eat and drink their way through. When he was telling his tale of woe to Calvin Johnson, the Transit Porter at the Howard Beach station, Calvin mentioned that he was throwing a birthday party for his son and could use some soda and candy. Leo welcomed the opportunity recoup some of his money, however small it may be, as well as to clear out a little space in his garage. He settled on a fair price with Calvin for an amount of soda and candy. The only problem now was getting the goods to Calvin at Howard Beach. Leo had already thrown away his money, so he had no intention of doing the same with his time by transporting the soda and candy to Calvin on his off-duty time. On his first train run in the morning he loaded several boxes of assorted candy and five cases of soda onto the Train to the Plane. He placed the boxes across the rear seats in the first car, a location where passengers rarely utilized.

When the train pulled out of 57th Street it was more crowded than usual, crowded enough where Leo was feeling a bit self-conscious because several passengers had to stand while his boxes lay across two seats. Leo stood directly next to his boxes, hoping no one would complain of their presence. When the train passed Jay Street an airline pilot slowly eased his way towards Leo. Leo could tell from the look in the man's eye that he intended to engage him in conversation. This was just great – not only was he about to get an earful about taking up seats on the train with his boxes, but the complaint was going to come from an airline pilot.

Leo steadied himself for the verbal barrage. The pilot pointed toward the boxes and looked directly at Leo. "Are those your boxes, officer?"

Leo nodded, "Yes, they are," he whispered. He took a deep breath and waited for the tirade to follow.

"How much for a snickers bar?" the pilot asked.

"What?" Leo was stunned.

"A snickers bar," the pilot repeated. "How much?"

"Oh, yeah, of course," Leo stammered. "fifty cents for a snickers bar."

"Here you go, my friend." The pilot handed Leo two quarters and removed a snickers bar from the top of the box.

Leo hadn't much time to digest the transaction before receiving a query from his right. "You have any chips in there?" the man asked. "I didn't have time to grab anything to eat this morning and I'm famished."

"Chips?" Leo said, "Sure, I have chips."

Two middle aged women jumped up and stood behind the man selecting his chips. "What a marvelous idea," one woman said to her companion. "Having snacks and drinks on the train."

"I think it's great," her friend replied, "and it's a long time coming."

When the Train to the Plane pulled into Howard Beach Leo was left with approximately half of what he had originally intended to give to Calvin. He was going to have to adjust his price, but he didn't care. A whole new business venture had appeared in front of him out of the blue.

For the next six months business was great for Leo Fromme. Not only was he able to completely clear out his garage stockpile, but he had to make another run to the wholesaler to stock up. He had his entire routine worked out perfectly. Every morning before his first train run he would carry some boxes onto the train and put them inside the empty conductor's cab at the rear of the first car. Once the train was underway and no sergeant was on board, he would break out his wares and the store was open for business. When the train reached Howard Beach, Leo would move his boxes back into the conductor's cab and wait until the train departed to bring them out again, or if he was taking a different train back to Manhattan, he would drag the boxes off the train and temporarily store them in Calvin Johnson's porter's room until his next train was ready to leave. Business was booming.

The end to this burgeoning empire came about from the most unlikely of sources. No one complained about the cop selling soda and candy on the Train to the Plane. To the contrary, the president's office of the Transit Authority received numerous letters commending the Authority for providing snacks and drinks on the train. The administrative assistant in the president's office was tasked with sending a letter of appreciation to the vendor who had the contract to sell snacks on the train. The president had assumed that such a vendor existed because only vendors with TA contracts could sell food or drink on transit property. When no authorized vendor could be found, the transit president contacted the MTA inspector general to look into the matter. From there, the situation developed quickly. The IG investigators notified the inspector general that a transit cop was selling soda and snacks on the Train to the Plane. The inspector general notified the president of the Transit Authority and the president notified the Chief of the Transit Police Department. The Chief of Department notified George Reed, the very personable Chief of Patrol. Lt. Beasley was visibly shaking when he departed Chief Reed's office. Rumor had it that the Chief swatted Beasley several times with his official Transit Police flyswatter.

For Leo Fromme, it was more lost money and another failed business venture. The lost money came from the official department charges he received along with the penalty of forfeiting thirty vacation days – a very serious financial hit. What bothered Leo most, however, was that the business had not really failed. In fact, he had stumbled on to a real money maker and had it pulled out from under him.

The day Leo came back from his suspension, Lt. Beasley went home sick in the middle of the day. It was widely rumored that the Lieutenant fell ill after Leo approached him and asked how he could go about applying for a permit to sell food on the Train to the Plane on his days off.

...

Doug Collins laughed out loud as he began typing. The saga of Leo Fromme was a perfect addition to the request for the unit citation.

CHAPTER 6: The Story of Police Officer Ludwig McGinn

When Ingrid Bauer came into the world in 1937, it was a life of culture and privilege that awaited her. Despite the constant beat of goose stepping Nazis, Berlin was still a center of culture. Ingrid's father was a professor at the University of Berlin, and her mother a violinist with a local orchestra. From the time Ingrid could handle a spoon to feed herself, her mother forced a violin bow into her hand. As the war heated up and eventually turned against Germany there was always the violin to serve as a distraction for Ingrid and her mother. Even during the bombing of Berlin and the Russian occupation, the sweet tones kept emanating from the shell of the Bauer's bombed out home.

The occupation was harsh, and Ingrid's father saw no future for his family in Russian controlled East Berlin. Every year since the war ended it was becoming increasingly difficult to cross over to West Berlin, so in 1953 Karl Bauer took his wife and sixteen-year-old daughter on the dangerous journey across the border to begin a new life in West Berlin.

Their apartment was tiny and Karl had to work manual labor jobs to provide for his family, but there was a peace of mind at being out from under the boot of Russian control that the family could not put a price tag on. The sweet melodies from Ingrid's violin seemed all the sweeter drifting through the free streets of West Berlin.

It was on that free street that U.S. Army private Patrick McGinn was patrolling when he stopped to listen to the hypnotic tones. He followed the sound until he found himself knocking on an apartment door.

In 1956 Patrick McGinn departed Europe on a transport ship for his return to the United States. He brought all his gear with him in his fully stuffed duffel bag, but he had one other possession that could not fit inside the bag – a pregnant wife.

Patrick and Ingrid settled in a small single-family house in Woodside, Queens. Whereas Ingrid had come from a family of privilege and culture, Patrick's background was blue collar to the core. His father was a hard-drinking construction worker and his mother was a housewife and caregiver for his six brothers and himself.

Patrick's dad recoiled when he learned his first grandson was named Ludwig McGinn, but he couldn't help but fawn over the baby just the same. Much to the chagrin of Ingrid, he even began calling the baby "Wiggy," a name that stuck with Ludwig into adulthood.

Aside from his rather odd sounding name, Ludwig McGinn was a paradox while growing up. On one hand, he was a typical New York City kid mixing it up on the streets with his gang of friends. On the other hand, however, was the cultured Ludwig, being trained daily as a classical violinist by his mother.

Ludwig loved his mother, but it wasn't just to humor her that he embraced the violin – he loved the violin. He was also street-smart enough to know that his love for the violin was something that had to remain a deep dark secret if he wanted to survive as a kid on the streets of New York.

Ludwig felt completely at peace when he played. There were things he could not express with words, but could only come out of him through the sound of his violin. There were times he felt his violin and he were one. His violin was his voice. The music came from his soul in the language everyone speaks before birth with no translation required.

When Ludwig graduated high school, he felt confident enough to come out of the closet with his musical skill. His father wanted him to get a college education, but he scoffed at the notion of going to college to pursue a musical career. With relentless harassment from Ingrid, Patrick finally gave in and gave his blessing to musical studies in college, with one condition. Patrick had come home from the Army and obtained a job as a mailman with the Post Office. He said he would support his son's college education but if he could not get a career in music, he would promise to take whatever tests Patrick told him to take in order to get a secure civil service job.

Ludwig and Ingrid happily agreed to the conditions and began planning Ludwig's college education. The Julliard School was extremely exclusive, with a microscopically small 8% of applicants being accepted. Ingrid realized there was good reason why Julliard was so exclusive. Simply put, it was one of the best music schools in the world, and as far as Ingrid was concerned, it was the only place for her son to study. There was a shockwave of enormous proportions registered within the McGinn household when the Julliard rejection letter was received. In retrospect, Ingrid should not have been so surprised. Ludwig was up against students who had already studied at the finest music schools in Manhattan. Even though Ludwig's training was likely better then more than half of these prodigies, as far as Julliard was concerned, Ludwig was a kid who had been taught to play the violin in his living room by his mother. The reality of the situation eased the pain when the rejection letter was received from the Manhattan School of Music, thought by many to be the second-best music school in the city behind Julliard.

Patrick McGinn privately breathed a huge sigh of relief when his son's college was announced. Patrick assumed that a quality music education meant an expensive education. In most cases, that was true, but the Aaron Copeland School of Music at Queens College was the exception. One of the oldest departments at Queens College, the school featured majors in general music, performance, and music education, all for City University of New York tuition that was a fraction of the cost for a private college.

Ingrid was less than enthusiastic about having her son trained at Queens College, but she did a complete about face when she toured the school and met the faculty. No matter which program they chose, all students took academic courses in theory, history, ear-training, sight-singing, performance, as well as private lessons.

The star of the school was their music building, which featured Steinway pianos in all practice rooms, a music library that had more than 35,000 scores, 30,000 books, and 20,000 recordings. Performances took place in Colden Auditorium, with its acoustics and the Maynard-Walker Memorial organ. The school produced over 300 concerts, including recitals, orchestra, choir, ensembles, new music, early music concerts, and opera productions.

It was the culmination of all his years of training and practice when Ludwig performed a solo in his senior year at a packed Colden Auditorium. As he took a bow to the standing ovation Ludwig could not imagine anything better – and he was right. It would not get any better.

Six months after graduation, disillusionment and depression had set in. It wasn't unexpected that Ludwig could not get an audition with the New York Philharmonic, but he couldn't get an audition with the American Symphony Orchestra either. He couldn't even get an audition with the Queens Symphony Orchestra, even though he was a graduate of Queens College.

When his father told him to take a seat in the living room, Ludwig knew what was coming.

"This is not a happy topic for me, Wiggy," Patrick began. "I know how much music means to you and it almost wants to make me cry."

"What wants to make you cry, dad?"

"Look at who you see living on the streets," Patrick said. "Many of those bums are musicians."

"Bums?" Ludwig recoiled.

Patrick held up his hands. "No offense meant, Wiggy. It's just a word I use." He cleared his throat. "The point is that you are lucky. There are plenty of out of work musicians who have no place to live, no car, no health insurance."

"What's your point, dad?"

"My point is that it's not your fault, Wiggy. You're a great fiddle player and I want you to go on fiddling."

Ludwig bit his lip and rolled his eyes. "It's a violin, dad."

"Whatever," Patrick replied. "But my point is that there are just too many of you music graduates and not enough jobs out there for musicians. There's comes a point when a man has to go out and make money."

"I have been making money," Ludwig snapped.

"How?"

"I've been busking."

"What the hell is busking?"

"I perform in front of the Met around closing time, and then walk over to Central Park for a while, then I go to Broadway and perform in front of a theatre, and then any other street with a busy sidewalk."

Patrick clasped his hand over his mouth. "Oh, my God! My son is a panhandler."

"I'm not a panhandler," Ludwig sighed. "I'm a street performer."

Patrick's face was turning red. "Call it what you want but it sounds like a bum to me."

"Hey," Ludwig fired back, "I'll bet this bum makes more money than you each day."

"Watch your tone with me boy," Patrick warned. He took a deep breath and nodded. "Let's just calm down and speak like reasonable men. Whatever money you're making you have to realize that this street performing is a dead end."

Ludwig shook his head. "Not necessarily. Besides the money to be made out there, there's a whole heap of different types of work that all involve playing music. So, what if it might not be my dream job. If I continue to play and get better, more opportunities will open up."

"I agree with you there," Patrick smirked. "Eventually, you'll qualify to be a waiter at an upscale restaurant rather than McDonalds."

"Do you have anything constructive to say?" Ludwig sighed.

"Of course," Patrick nodded. "I'm here to remind you about our agreement from four and a half years ago. You agreed that if you didn't have a secure job after you graduated college, you would take some civil service tests."

"Well, I don't want to be a mailman," Ludwig groaned.

"You don't have to be a mailman," Patrick replied. "I signed you up for a test for transit police officer."

"A cop in the subway?" Ludwig gasped.

"They make good money and they have great benefits." Patrick smiled. "It's the kind of job you can start a family with and keep right on fiddling if you choose."

In 1980, an enthusiastic Patrick McGinn watched his less than enthusiastic son graduate from the Police Academy. After graduation Ludwig increased the frequency of his violin practice. He still loved the violin and he found playing to be a soothing distraction from the stress of being a cop patrolling the subway.

Two things happened in 1985 that had an impact on Ludwig's career. First, he was assigned to the uniformed citywide task force. He was only in the assignment for two weeks when he was moved into the Train to the Plane Unit. The rumor was that Ludwig had a big hook to enable someone with only five years on the job to get on the Train to the Plane. The reality, however, was quite different. The roster for the Train to the Plane Unit was a man short, and there were no new applicants cleared for the assignment. The administrative sergeant in the task force took the simplest solution and moved the last cop assigned to the task force into the Train to the Plane Unit. Ludwig didn't mind. His heart had never been into police work, so he would just assume ride the train back and forth between Manhattan and Queens.

The second happening of 1985 was the establishment of MUNY. It was then that the MTA Arts & Design began managing the Music

Under New York program, to bring joyous and engaging music to the commuting public.

Prohibition of musical performance in the New York City subway was common since the MTA's early history. Some musicians still sang and played instruments in an effort to earn money, but they risked receiving a summons or even being arrested. Following a court order challenge by musician Roger Manning, in 1985, the ban on subway performance was declared unconstitutional and the MTA created MUNY.

Music Under New York artists were guaranteed the same rights as other street performers in New York. However, association with MUNY provided benefits to performers like priority scheduling in popular locations, access to commuter railroad terminals, and fewer problems with law enforcement.

Auditions were held in Grand Central and were judged by a panel of professionals from the music industry. Ludwig received the highest possible scores for his five-minute performance based on "quality, variety, and appropriateness, for the mass transit environment."

Ludwig was more upbeat that he had been since he became a transit cop. He already had a plan in his head. He worked steady 6 a.m. to 2 p.m. with Sundays and Mondays as regular days off. He would perform at his authorized location on his days off and also in the late afternoons and evenings after work whenever he felt up to it. Finally, he was going to play regularly for an audience at an authorized location.

Ludwig's plan crashed and burned when he was summoned into Lt. Beasley's office.

"You submitted a request for off duty employment." Beasley said.

"That's correct, sir," Ludwig nodded.

"Well, your request is denied," Beasley snapped.

"What?"

"You heard me," Beasley snarled, "Your request is denied."

"But why?" Ludwig pled.

"Are you a moron?" Beasley smirked. "A transit cop can't get a permit to perform work on transit property."

"But, I wouldn't be getting paid by transit."

"But you'd be accepting money from transit passengers, right?"

Ludwig shrugged. "I guess so."

"Go fiddle on your own time." Beasley picked up the newspaper on his desk. "You are dismissed, officer."

Ludwig was seething. He never particularly liked being a cop and he never cared for Lt. Beasley. Now, he hated his boss, and his hate only seemed to grow as days passed. He kept remembering his father's speech warning him that he needed a good secure job before he could start a family. Here he was almost six years later with his secure job, but he was still living at home with his parents with no girlfriend and no prospects of starting a family. What the hell did he need this security for. All he ever wanted to do in life was perform with his violin, and suddenly, a great avenue for performance opened up in front of him only to be shut down by his jerk off lieutenant.

Several weeks passed and still Ludwig's mood did not improve. The only time he felt at peace was home in his room playing his violin. Then one evening when he returned his violin to its case and idea formed that would allow him the same feeling of peace while working.

The next morning at 6:30 a.m. everything was running according to the routine. Ludwig stood watch by the lone open door of the train as the conductor collected the fares for the Train to the Plane. The early morning passengers quietly found seats. The commuters actually heading to the airport stowed their luggage in the overhead racks while those using the train as a convenience paged through newspapers or closed their eyes for a nap. The two tones signaled the closing door, and the whoosh of the air brake was followed by the initial jerk of the train as it slowly rolled forward.

Ludwig moved to the back of the train and stood in front of the locked conductor's cab. The train rocked rhythmically as it picked up speed. Everyone seemed quiet and content. No one noticed Ludwig grab his key ring, or disappear inside the conductor's cab. No one noticed when he reappeared in the car carrying something he did not have when he entered the cab. The first time anyone took notice of Ludwig was when the soothing tones of Beethoven's Violin Sonata No. 9 filled the car. Everyone was mesmerized, including the conductor. When the train stopped to pick up additional passengers, Ludwig briefly paused to make sure a sergeant wasn't boarding. Then he was right back into his beautiful melodies. When the train arrived at Howard beach Ludwig received an ovation from everyone on the train, with some passengers stopping to tell him it was the best experience they ever had on the subway.

Ludwig began conducting his on-board concerts every day he worked, and they had the desired effect. The performances made him feel good. In fact, for the first time he looked forward to going to work. About three weeks into his performance run, there were additional passengers on his first train. It was a reporter and film crew from a local TV station. The pretty reporter walked up to Ludwig and asked if he was the violin-playing cop. Ludwig froze for a moment to consider his response. The safe answer would be to say that he didn't know what she was talking about. On the other hand, there was a TV camera ten feet away that was there to film his performance. He took a deep breath and admitted that he was the cop they were seeking. "What the hell," he thought. A chance to perform on TV is a once in a lifetime opportunity for a violinist, even if it did get him in trouble with the Transit Police and Lt. Beasley.

Ludwig never performed better and when the train reached Howard Beach the reporter had a tear in her eye as she declared Ludwig as being magnificent. Ludwig rushed home that afternoon, but there was really no need to hurry. He usually got home before 4 p.m. and the reporter told him his piece would run sometime during the five o'clock news. At five o'clock Ludwig had his parents seated on the living room couch waiting for the big surprise he promised on the television. It was at exactly 5:27 when the story aired. Ingrid wept openly watching her son perform. Even Patrick's eyes began to well up at the sight of his son on TV. The story was over at 5:30 at which time mother, father, and son shared an embrace. The tender moment was disrupted at 5:31 by a phone call. Ludwig was directed to report to the Chief of Patrol's office at 7 a.m. the next morning.

Ludwig had never met Chief of Patrol George Reed personally, but he knew of his immense size and surly reputation. It was with much trepidation that he eased his way into the Chief's office. The Chief looked even larger behind his huge oak desk. He took off his reading glasses and leaned back in his chair. "I guess you think you're pretty cute, don't you Beethoven?" Reed growled.

"I'm not sure what you mean," Ludwig stammered.

"You're full of shit," Reed snapped, "but that doesn't matter. For that stunt you pulled I either have to beat your ass or commend you."

Reed slowly rose from his chair allowing Ludwig to take in the reality of his immense size. Ludwig gulped as he tried to interpret whether the aforementioned ass kicking was figurative or literal. Ludwig's breaths became more rapid as the Chief moved out from behind his desk and advanced, raising his right hand as he drew closer. Ludwig braced himself for the worst. It looked like the threat was going to be literal. Ludwig bit his lip and tensed his muscles in preparation of an impact, but none came. Instead, the Chief's right hand hung in front of him in anticipation of a handshake. Ludwig's hand was lost inside the huge mitt, and his shoulder nearly dislocated from the shaking.

Finally, the Chief released his grip. "Sit down, officer."

Ludwig plopped in the chair, still trying to control his breathing.

"I can't tell you how many phone calls we got after your little concert last night," Reed began. "Everyone loved it. Even the Mayor, Police Commissioner, and the President of the Transit Authority called to say how wonderful you were." Reed sunk back behind his desk and shrugged. "And if they think you're wonderful, I think you're wonderful."

There was a buzzing from the Chief's phone prompting him to push down a button. "Yeah? Well get him in here."

The office door opened and Lt. Beasley entered. He was obviously out of breath, but the Chief gave him no opportunity to talk anyway. "You must be here for the 7:10 meeting, Lieutenant. Officer McGinn and I are here for the 7:00 meeting."

"I'm so sorry, Chief," Beasley gasped, "but the traffic..."

"Traffic!" Reed erupted. "This is the God damn Transit Police. Why didn't you take the train?"

Beasley attempted to change the spotlight of blame away from himself and on to someone else. "I'm very sorry Chief, and I'm also sorry for the outrageous actions of this officer. How dare he have the gall to pull a stunt like that on the train. At your direction I will suspend him from duty and remove his shield and firearm right now."

"Shut up, you moron," Reed bellowed, "while I tell you exactly what you are going to do."

"Yes, sir," Beasley whispered.

"Everyone loves what this officer did so I love what this officer did," Reed said.

"I love what the officer did too, sir," Beasley sniveled. "He's one of my best men."

"Be quiet before I take my flyswatter to the side of your head again." Reed pointed his huge index finger directly at Beasley's nose. "This is exactly what you are going to do. You are going to allow this officer two hours during every tour to perform."

Beasley tried to respond, "But I don't think..."

"You're coming dangerously close to a swatting," Reed warned. "I want the officer to have a place set up right outside District 1 at Columbus Circle where he can perform during the last two hours of his shift. You will set up some type of donation bucket for him and any money collected will go to the police widows and orphans fund." Reed turned toward Ludwig. "How does that sound, officer?"

"It sounds fantastic, sir," Ludwig beamed.

Beasley held up his hand. "If you don't mind me saying, sir, I think this is a huge mistake."

The sneer on Reed's face grew as he addressed Ludwig. "Get out of here officer and prepare for you next performance. I have some more business with your lieutenant."

"Yes, sir," Ludwig nodded before reaching behind him and grabbing the door knob. As he closed the door behind him and began moving down the hall he heard distinct slapping sounds coming from the Chief's office, sounds consistent with a flyswatter smacking human flesh. He hoped and prayed that his analysis of the sounds was correct.

...

When Doug finished reading the report he was momentarily puzzled. This story was a positive achievement for the unit. Why would Beasley bury it in the incident binder? Doug smiled and nodded. Of course, Beasley wanted to draw as little attention as possible to his swatting from Chief Reed. Doug began typing on the unit citation request report. Beasley's thrashing alone was enough for inclusion in the unit citation request.

CHAPTER 7: The Story of Police Officer Nick Montgomery

Although they probably won't admit it, most parents of twins panic when they bring their babies home with the fear that they will misidentify their children. This fear is not present in parents of fraternal twins – only in identical twins. That's because identical twins result from one fertilized egg splitting into two during pregnancy. When they're born, identical twins share the same DNA, which explains why they usually look almost exactly alike and why parents tremble at the thought of going through life calling their children by the wrong names.

Doctors try to alleviate parental fears by explaining that even though identical twins come from the same sperm and egg, and have the same chromosomes and genes, there are environmental differences that can affect the way they look and behave. For example, one twin may have been positioned in the womb in a way that he got more nutrients or blood supply and may be born larger than the other. The twins may have had different childhood illnesses as they grew up. They may have different lifestyles – exercise, smoking, drinking, nutrition, job stress, etc. As identical twins get older they may look more and more different, because they are exposed to more diverse environments. Additionally, they pointed to the science of epigenetics to explain how these environmental influences can affect the genes. As a result of the environment, chemicals called "epigenetic marks" attach to the chromosomes and can turn specific genes on or off. So identical twins with identical DNA may have different genes turned on, causing them to look and act differently, and even to develop different diseases such as cancer. That's what the doctors said, but as far as Ann and Joe Montgomery were concerned, their boys were exact Xerox copies of each other and they couldn't tell them apart without some help.

Ann's solution was to color code her boys. For Nick and Patrick, she used red and green. She dressed Nick in red for St. Nick and Patrick in green for St. Patrick. This system not only helped her and her husband but was invaluable for helping others tell the twins apart, especially in daycare or school situations. It was also helpful when they took photographs. Looking back, they were always able to tell who was who in a photo.

As a failsafe, Ann placed a dab of nail polish on the little toe of Nick's right foot, a practice she continued until Nick finally refused to accept the nail polish at the age of eight.

Aside from the misidentification fears, the twins were a joy for the Montgomery's. In their childhood and pre-teen years they were never any problem for their parents and they were inseparable. There was something about the boys that was like a happy summer day, as if they reflected the warmth of one another, and passed it like a beach-ball if the other felt sadness. Perhaps that's what made them so resilient and such a joy to be around. There were, of course, times they fought, but then they were simply as puppies learning how to be dogs and the hostility evaporated as quickly as it came.

Then, the teenage years set in and all the doctor's theories regarding differences came to pass - not physical differences. As the boys moved through puberty and into manhood they still looked exactly the same, but they had developed vastly different personalities. Nick was serious, cautious and goal oriented, with his sights set on establishing a career and family. Patrick, on the other hand, was a carefree spirit who looked no further into the future than the next night at the neighborhood bar. By the time 1985 rolled around these two brothers who looked so much alike had travelled vastly different paths.

Nick had served a tour of duty with the Army in Vietnam before coming home and putting his plan into action. Within two years he had a wife, a new baby boy and a small house on Long island. He also had a secure job as a New York City Transit Police Officer. By 1985

Nick had three kids, eleven years on the job and was assigned to the Train to the Plane Unit.

Patrick had barely graduated high school and when his number came up high in the draft lottery he hit the road to Canada. He remained in Toronto until 1977, when President Carter issued a presidential proclamation granting amnesty to those who evaded the draft. During his time in Canada Patrick's existence consisted of drinking in bars, smoking pot, and living off the salary he made from performing odd jobs as well as the money his parents sent him every month. Back in the United States Patrick's lifestyle didn't change much. In 1985, Patrick worked from time to time at a cash wash, and lived with his parents. He spent most of his time at the neighborhood bar getting drunk and smoking pot.

Nick loved his twin brother but considered him a lost cause, but not the type of lost cause that he didn't want to associate with. He still had Patrick over to his house on birthdays and holidays and his kids loved their uncle Patrick. Nick was at peace with the fact that Patrick was set in his ways and that there was nothing he would be able to do to change him.

If there was one benefit to their completely different lifestyles, no one had any trouble telling these identical twins apart anymore. They were still the same height, weight, and build, but Nick was clean shaven with a short, military style haircut while Patrick sported long, stringy hair with a scruffy beard.

August 1985 was a huge month in the life of the Montgomery family. They were going away on a family vacation, and for the first time they were flying to Florida to Disneyworld. Nick had Sunday and Monday as regular days off and was able to get a vacation pick for the week they were going to Disney. To get the best deal on this vacation Nick's booked a flight for his family that departed on Saturday morning. Saturday was a scheduled work day for Nick, but he didn't foresee a problem with his plan. He requested a personal day off on

Saturday to be followed by his regular days off of Sunday and Monday. His vacation days would cover from Tuesday to Saturday. Their return flight was booked for Saturday giving Nick two days to unwind and recuperate before returning to work on Tuesday. Nick had every detail of the vacation worked out, except for one small item. That item threw his life into disarray three days before his scheduled departure.

Nick stood at the doorway to the office. "You wanted to see me, Lieutenant?"

"Yeah, come in Montgomery," Lt. Beasley said as he closed the newspaper on his desk.

"What can I do for you, sir?" Nick asked.

Beasley scanned his desktop before grabbing a TP-20 - the form used by a police officer requesting a day off. "You put in a TP-20 for Saturday."

"That's right," Nick smiled. "I'm taking the family to Disney. It's the first time we're going there."

Beasley extended the form to Nick. "Well, your request to have Saturday off is denied."

Nick was stunned. "What?" he gasped.

"If I give you off, I'll be going over the allotted quota for excusals for the day."

"But everyone goes over the quota," Nick blurted. "It's not a big deal."

"It is to me," Beasley replied. "Some supervisors don't care about the rules, but I have never approved an over-quota excusal, and I'm damn proud of that."

"But Lieutenant," Nick pled. "My flight leaves on Saturday morning. If I can't have off on Saturday it ruins the entire vacation."

"You should have thought of that before you just assumed you would be able to get Saturday off. You know what happens when you assume," he smirked. "You make an ass of you and me."

Nick's face had turned beet red. "Let me worry about making an ass of myself, and you do a damn good job already of making an ass of yourself."

"You're way out of line, officer," Beasley shouted. "And don't even think about calling in sick Saturday. I will make sure a sick investigator visits your house to make sure you are home."

Nick didn't hang around to hear anymore threats. He was out of the office and the district and onto the mezzanine. He had much bigger problems than soothing Beasley's ego. What was he going to do about his vacation?

Desperate times call for desperate actions and Nick had sunk to the bottom of the desperation barrel when he entered the Drunken Saint. Besides having the reputation for being the most degenerate, dive bar on Long Island, the Drunken Saint was the first place to look for Patrick Montgomery, and he didn't disappoint his brother. Nick was already settled on the adjacent stool before Patrick noticed him.

"Hey Paddy," he greeted as he slapped his brother on the shoulder.

"Good God!" Patrick declared as he wheeled away from his conversate with a very drunk female. "What a surprise. It's my big brother."

Although they were identical twins Patrick always referred to Nick as his big brother because Nick was first to come out of the womb.

"What brings you into this den of iniquity?" Patrick chuckled.

Nick's lips curled into a smile. "I was missing my brother, isn't that enough?"

"I may be drunk, but I'm not stupid," Patrick howled.

"Okay, okay," Nick conceded. "I'm in a tight spot and I need your help."

Patrick placed both hands over his heart. "Did I just hear you correctly because I think my heart just stopped. You need my help?"

"That's right, Paddy. I've thought this through a million ways and I came up with only one solution to my dilemma."

Patrick draped his arm around his brother and called out to the bartender. "Hey Sean, give my brother a beer." He then turned toward Nick. "Now, tell Paddy Boy your troubles."

"I'm leaving Saturday with the family for a vacation at Disney."

"What's the problem?" Patrick asked. "Do you want me to go in your place?"

"Heaven forbid," Nick said before taking a sip of beer. He wiped his mouth with his hand and wagged his index finger at Patrick. "But you're on the right track."

"What's that supposed to mean?"

This time it was Nick draping his arm around Patrick's shoulder. "Listen, Paddy, I have next week off as vacation but we're flying out Saturday morning so I had to take Saturday off as an additional personal day."

"So?" Patrick said, "What's the big deal?"

"The big deal is that my scumbag lieutenant is denying my day off for Saturday."

"Give him a smack in the head," Patrick suggested.

"Believe me," Nick sighed, "I'd love to but it doesn't work that way in the real world."

"So, how can I help you, Nicky?"

"I need you to be me for the day," Nick blurted.

"What?" Patrick gasped. "You want me to be a cop?" He waved his hands in front of him. "Forget it. That's too crazy – even for me."

"No, no, listen to me Paddy," Nick urged. "This can work. Trust me."

Patrick shrugged and held his arms out to the side. "But I don't know anything about being a cop."

Nick shook his head. "You don't have to. This unit I'm in is the Train to the Plane Unit. All I do is ride the train from Midtown Manhattan into Howard Beach Queens where passengers get a shuttle bus to the airport. That's all I do. The bosses don't want us getting off the train to take any police actions."

"That's it?" Patrick asked. "That's all you do?"

"That's it," Nick confirmed.

Patrick shook his head. "I should have taken that test. Even I can do a job like that."

"Then you'll do it?" Nick asked.

Patrick shrugged. "How could I let my big brother down."

"Great!" Nick slapped his brother on the back. "Now, we have a lot of details to take care of."

Patrick's eyes narrowed. "What details?"

"First of all," Nick began, "I have to take you for a haircut."

"A haircut?" Patrick shrieked.

"That's right," Nick nodded. "Don't you think it would be a little suspicious if I grew long hair and a beard overnight?"

"Possibly," Patrick shrugged.

"Look," Nick explained, "I'm not gonna ask you to do all this for nothing. I'll give you the day's pay I would have received."

"Don't insult me, Nicky," Patrick grinned. "It doesn't take money to get me to help you."

"That's very nice of you," Nick nodded.

"However," Patrick continued, "an appropriate donation to my favorite charity may be in order."

"And just what charity are you talking about?"

Patrick's lips curled into a huge smile. "Me!"

•••

Nick bounced up from his leaning position against the hood of his car and moved to greet Patrick as he exited the barber shop. "If I didn't know any better I would say I'm looking into a mirror," he declared.

Patrick was less enthusiastic. "I have to tell you, Nicky, this haircut of yours isn't very stylish. I may have to stay home until it grows back."

"That wouldn't be the worst thing in the world," Nick snickered.

"What's next?" Patrick asked.

"Now, we go to my garage and see how you look all suited up."

"Your garage?" Patrick questioned. "Why don't we go into your house?"

"I haven't said a word to Joanne about this scheme and she may be home."

"So, what if she's home," Patrick commented.

"My wife is not all that crazy about you, and the last thing I need is for her to find out that you are impersonating me while we fly to Florida."

Forty-five minutes later Nick sat on a bench in his garage and nodded. "I'm glad I never kept my New Year's resolution and began working out," he said. "We have the exact same pot belly."

"Aside from your stupid jokes, how do I look?" Patrick asked.

"My uniform fits you like a glove," Nick responded.

Patrick glided over to a mirror in the corner of the garage. "I look pretty good as a cop, don't you think?"

"Don't get carried away with yourself," Nick cautioned.

Patrick turned towards Nick and grabbed the butt of the holstered revolver. "Who knows? I may get to plug some dirtbag." Patrick came out of his dramatic crouch and kept tugging on the gun butt. "Hey, how come this gun won't come out of the holster?"

"There's a lock on the holster," Nick replied.

"How does the lock work?"

Nick waved his hand. "Oh, no. That's information you have no need to know. As a matter of fact," he continued, "I'm taking the bullets out of the gun before I unleash you."

"What If someone gets the drop on me out there?" Patrick asked.

"Surrender!" Nick responded.

"That's no fun," Patrick lamented.

Nick pointed to the bench across from him. "Shut up and sit down. I have a lot to brief you on."

Patrick dropped onto the bench. "Fire away, boss."

"Okay, then," Nick began. "I'll pick you up at five o'clock Saturday morning."

"Five o'clock?" Patrick moaned.

"That's right," Nick replied. "Now shut up and listen. When I pick you up you'll be in this full uniform. I'll drive you into Manhattan and drop you off at Columbus Circle. I'll take you right up to the subway stairs that are closest to District 1."

"I've never been to District 1," Patrick remarked. "How will I find it?"

"When you come out from the stairway you'll be staring at the district door directly across the mezzanine. Train to the Plane cops don't stand a formal roll call so you just walk into the district and nod and smile at the cop and sergeant behind the desk. To the right of the desk officer on a shelf is a log book that has JFK printed in whiteout on its cover. Go to the log book and sign in. Remember to use military time."

"I wasn't in the military," Patrick said.

"Don't be stupid," Nick snapped. "Write 0630 P.O. Montgomery PFD."

Patrick grinned. "What's PFD – pretty far out dude?"

Nick grit is teeth and looked at the floor. "No, it means present for duty."

"Got it, chief," Patrick said.

Nick pointed at his brother. "Remember, sign my name, not your name."

"10-4," Patrick laughed. "See, I know cop talk."

"Right next to that log book is another log book labelled radio log, and to the right of the log will be a bunch of portable radios in chargers. Take a radio and look at the number labelled on its front. Find that number in the log and sign my name next to it in the radio log."

"Where do I keep the radio?" Patrick asked.

Nick pointed to the left side of the gun belt. "You see that empty case on the belt – that's for the radio. You slide it in and snap it to secure it." Nick took a deep breath. "Make sure the radio is turned on and then don't touch it for the rest of the day. The only time you would ever think of pulling it out is if they were calling you."

"How would I know they are calling me?"

Nick pointed to Patrick's left breast. "You see the shield?"

"Yeah," Patrick nodded.

"You see the number on the shield?"

Patrick looked down as he tilted the shield up. "4878."

"The radio operator would say 'JFK shield 4878 on the air.' That is the only call you should even consider answering, understand?"

"Understood."

"Once you sign in and get a radio you will walk out of the command and go to your train."

"Where's the train?"

"I'm gonna take you there tomorrow night," Nick said, "so you'll know exactly where to go. Once you get on the train," Nick continued, "just stand in the back of the train and do nothing."

"Is that what you do?" Patrick asked.

"That's right," Nick said. "I do nothing except ride the train back and forth."

"Where do I get a job like that?" Patrick scoffed.

"That's a tough one for you, my brother," Nick shot back, "because you seem to have trouble finding any job."

"Very funny," Patrick groaned.

"Listen," Nick continued, "My Saturday schedule is simple. You ride the first train from 57th Street to Howard Beach. You stay on the same train and ride it back to 57th Street. Then you continue to stay on the train and go back to Howard Beach again. This time you get off the train at Howard Beach because it's time for your meal period."

"Where can I get something to eat at Howard Beach?" Patrick asked.

"Forget that," Nick said. "You're not leaving the station. The last thing I want to risk is you getting involved in some police action while walking in the street."

"Then where am I supposed to go?"

Nick pointed to the gun belt Patrick was wearing. "Give me my key ring."

There were at least thirty keys on the ring. Nick flipped through the keys until he found the one he was looking for. All the other keys dangled below the one he held between his index finger and thumb. "This is a 400 key," he said. "It opens most locks on the system."

"It looks like all the other keys on that ring," Patrick noted.

"You're right," Nick agreed, "but if you look close you will see a dab of white out on this key. When you get off the train at Howard Beach for your meal period, I want you to go up the stairs to the mezzanine and walk towards the token booth. When you approach the booth, smile and wave at the clerk. She's gonna know why you're coming over. She's gonna walk to the corner of the booth to your left and pull the bolt that unlocks a small compartment in the corner of the booth. There's a phone behind that small door. You're gonna use the phone to call out to meal.

"Who do I call?"

"Don't worry," Nick assured, "I'll have everything written out for you on a piece of paper, including the phone number to District 1" He cleared his throat. "Anyway, you call the number and when the cop or sergeant at the District 1 desk answers you say, 'Montgomery out to meal at Howard beach.' That's it – don't say anything more. Don't comment on the weather or anything else."

Patrick saluted officiously. "Yes, sir."

Nick shook his head. "I'm obviously out of my mind for trying to pull this off." He took a deep breath. "When you hang up the phone, you will make an about face. In the corner of the mezzanine you'll see a door with a padlock on it. That's the porter's room. The 400 key opens the lock and the room is relatively clean with a comfortable chair inside. Sit in that room and don't move until your next train."

"You expect me to sit in a dirty little subway hole in the wall for an hour," Patrick moaned.

"Actually," Nick sighed. "It's more like two and a half hours."

"What?"

"Your meal period is an hour, but your next scheduled train out of Howard Beach isn't for two and a half hours. Technically, you're supposed to patrol the station for an hour and a half, but I want you to stay in that room." Nick held up his right index finger. "The only time I want you to come out of that room is when the hour is up you go back to the booth."

"Let me guess," Patrick broke in. "I go to the same phone – dial the same number and say that I'm off my meal period."

"You're catching on," Nick nodded. "Then go back into the porter's room until it's time for your train run. Don't worry about the train runs. I'll have the times written out for you."

"Okay," Patrick said, "how do I finish up my time as Johnny law?"

Nick sighed. "This is the most dangerous part. When you get off that last train at 57th Street you go up to the street and walk to Columbus Circle. Make believe you're wearing blinders when you walk. In other words, don't get involved in anything! When you get to Columbus Circle, go down the same stairs where I dropped you off and go into District 1."

Patrick held up his hand. "Let me see if I can take it from here. I put the radio back where I found it and sign the radio log."

"Correct," Nick nodded.

"Then I sign that other log with PFD again."

"Not quite," Nick corrected. "This time you sign my name and put EOT after it."

Patrick placed his hand on his forehead and closed his eyes. "Don't tell me. Everything Over Today."

"End of tour," Nick sighed.

"That was pretty close," Patrick grinned.

"Forget that," Nick snapped. "There's one more detail. Your street clothes will be stashed in my locker. Once you sign the logs and put the radio back you keep walking to the right. You will pass through the muster room and the next door is the male locker room. When you reach the third row of lockers you turn right and look for my name on the front of a locker. You will have my combination, so you open the locker and hang up my uniform shirt and pants – put the shoes in the bottom of the locker – the hat on the top shelf, and the gun belt on the hook. Your clothes and sneakers will be in a bag in the locker."

Patrick rocked back on the bench and slapped his thighs. "Okay, I guess that's it."

"Almost," Nick replied. "He reached into his pocket and pulled out what looked like a small notepad. "This is my memo book. You have to have this on you while you're working and you are required to make entries throughout the shift."

"How am I going to know what entries to make?"

"I will have the book filled out for you with the entries you need to go on duty and I will have written out for you the entries you need to make and the times you need to make them."

"Why don't you just write all the crap in the book for me?" Patrick asked.

Nick shook his head. "I can't. You may see a sergeant during the day and he is going to sign your book. If a sergeant walks up on you, salute and hand him the memo book. Tell him everything is okay and don't say anything more."

"Is that finally everything?" Patrick asked.

"For you, yes," Nick answered.

"What do you still have to do?" Patrick inquired.

"Once I drop you off right now, I have to stop at Saint Aiden's and say some prayers to Saint Jude." Nick said.

"Who is Saint Jude?"

"The patron saint of lost causes."

Patrick stood up and stretched. "Oh, ye of little faith. Have no fear Nicky, your little brother will have everything under control."

...

Nick eased his Chevy Celebrity head into the space near the subway stairs. He shifted into park and turned in the seat to face Patrick. "Okay, this is it," he declared. "It's show time. Please don't mess this up or I will be totally screwed."

"I got this, Nicky," Patrick grinned.

Nick looked at his watch. "It's 6:15 – perfect timing for you to go down and sign in."

Patrick opened the passenger door. "Okay, away I go."

Nick grabbed his arm. "Wait!" he eyed Patrick up and down. "You have the full uniform on. Do you have the written instructions I gave you?"

Patrick reached into his right pants pocket and displayed a folded piece of paper. "Check," he said.

Patrick emerged from the stairway brimming with confidence. Based on the tour Nick had given him the day before he knew exactly where District 1 was located. He walked across the mezzanine with a swagger befitting the saltiest veteran. On an early Saturday morning there was only a sprinkling of riders scurrying in all directions, but one of those sprinkles – a middle age woman – was drawn to that cop magnet uniform.

"Excuse me, officer."

It took a moment for Patrick to realize he was the officer. Finally, he turned and struck an officious pose with his arms folder across his chest. "What's up, lady?"

"How do I get to the Statue of Liberty?" she asked.

Patrick removed his hat and scratched his head. "That's a good question."

There was an awkward moment of silence before the woman followed up. "Well, do you have a good answer?"

"Yeah," Patrick said. "Your best bet is to go upstairs and take a cab."

"What?" the woman gasped. "Don't you know how to get there by train?"

Patrick shook his head. "No, I never been there before," he calmly replied.

"This is outrageous," the woman huffed. "You're a police officer."

"That's right, lady," Patrick fired back, "I'm a police officer, not a map. I'm sure there's plenty of places I could ask you directions for and you wouldn't know."

The woman leaned in closer to get a look at the nametag on the uniform shirt. "Thanks for nothing, Officer Montgomery, and you can be sure I'll be writing a letter to the mayor about your outrageous behavior."

"Tell him I voted for him," Patrick called as the woman stormed off.

Patrick turned and eyed the door of District 1. "Okay," he whispered, "on with the mission."

Billy Bob Harris was a Transit Police legend. The white haired 32-year veteran and native of Alabama still wore the high and tight haircut of a Marine, and for good reason. Harris had been awarded the Medal of Honor for action during the Korean War. For the last twenty-three years, the gruff, no-nonsense sergeant had been working steady midnights at District 1. Harry Brenner was also a District 1 veteran, having worked as the steady midnight assistant desk officer for more than ten years. When Patrick pushed through the door, as was his custom, desk officer Billy Bob never looked up to acknowledge the entrant.

Harry Brenner however, was about as affable a fellow as could be found. "Good morning, Nick," Harry chirped from his seat next to Sergeant Harris.

Patrick eyed the log books and radios to the right but was going to maintain proper social decorum by acknowledging the greeting. "How's it hanging, boys," he sang as he passed by the desk.

The greeting got Billy Bob's attention. "What the...what did he just say?"

Harry knew exactly what was said, but he knew better than to tell. Instead, he shrugged. "I'm not sure, sarge."

"Who was that, anyway?" Billy Bob asked.

"Nick Montgomery from the JFK Unit," Harry replied.

Billy Bob returned to his paperwork while Harry held his breath as he saw Patrick approaching. He hoped he would just depart the district without uttering a word, but in Patrick's mind, that would be rude.

"Don't take any wooden nickels, boys," Patrick said as he opened the district door.

Harry closed his eyes and grit his teeth as Billy Bob exploded. "Hey you," he yelled. "Who the hell do you think you're talking to like that?"

Patrick remained in the doorway holding the door open. "Easy Whitey," he said. "You're gonna pop a blood vessel."

Billy Bob sat behind the desk with his face beet red, his eyes as wide as silver dollars and his mouth wide open, but for the moment he was incapable of speech. Patrick moved through the door but not before imparting some final words of wisdom. "You should start meditating, Whitey. It worked wonders for me." And with that, he was gone.

Billy Bob continued staring straight ahead at the closed district door. Thirty seconds went by before Harry felt it necessary to check on his sergeant. "Are you okay, sarge?"

Billy Bob slowly turned and looked at Harry. He took a deep breath. "I'm going to erase the last five minutes from my mind." He then looked down and continued with his paperwork.

Patrick was not yet settled in the passenger seat before being questioned by Nick. "Did everything go alright?"

Patrick stared straight ahead. "A piece of cake," he declared. "If the rest of the day goes like this we got it made in the shade."

Five minutes later Nick pulled to the curb next to the subway stairs for the 57th Street station. He leaned back in the driver's seat and took a deep breath. "Okay, I guess that's it. I have to hurry home and get everyone to the airport."

"Didn't your wife say anything when you said you had to go out a few hours before you're leaving for Florida?"

"I told her I left my wallet in my uniform pants so I had to drive to District 1 to get it."

Patrick walked around to the driver's side and extended his hand through the window. "Have a great vacation Nicky."

"Thanks, Paddy. Have a good day and then go back to the bar and get drunk."

"You don't have to worry about that," Patrick chuckled as he slammed the passenger door closed. When he reached the top of the stairs he turned back toward the car. "That was pretty good using your wallet as an excuse," he called. "I'll have to remember that if I ever get married."

Nick watched his brother disappear down the subway stairs. He shifted into drive, but before he made any movement he looked up to the roof of the car. "Please, Saint Jude, let this work out today."

Patrick marched right to the platform Nick had taken him to the day before, and sure enough, there it was. The illuminated blue circle in the window of the lead car contained the white outline of an airplane. Patrick had found his destination – the Train to the Plane.

Patrick boarded the train through the single open door. "Good morning," conductor Melvin Perkins greeted as he set up his ticket and cash table inside the train.

Melvin dropped some quarters on the floor when Patrick returned the greeting. "Good morning brother man."

As directed, Patrick marched to the rear of the car and turned to face the riders. The hard part was over. He was on post and all he had to do now was ride the train.

Nick had said that the Saturday trains were pretty light. There were only twelve passengers on the train when Melvin's voice rang out over the train PA system. "This is the JFK express to Howard Beach and Kennedy Airport." Melvin's voice was followed by the high – low tones indicating the train door was closing.

As the door closed Patrick could hear a high pitch shriek from the platform. "Wait, please." The voice quickly faded as the door shut. A moment later the door opened and a breathless new passenger boarded the train.

Patrick was mesmerized. The gorgeous lady had the statuesque figure of a runway model and she seemed to glow in her red flight attendant uniform and golden blonde hair.

"Thank you so much," the flight attendant puffed.

"No problem, Gwen," Melvin smiled.

The high-low tones sounded again, but this time the doors remained closed as the train jerked into motion. The breathless flight attendant walked to the rear of the car and smiled widely at Patrick as she settled into a seat. "How are you today?" she said.

"Much better now that I've seen you, beautiful," Patrick replied.

"Oh, okay," Gwen said as her face took on expression as if she had just smelled something very bad.

"Where are you flying off to, sweetie?" Patrick asked.

The bad smell expression remained on Gwen's face. "I have a quick hop to Miami. I'll be home by seven o'clock tonight."

"Great," Patrick grinned. "So, we'll have plenty of time to get busy tonight."

Gwen squinted and curled her lip. "Is everything okay, Nick."

"What's wrong?" Patrick asked.

"I see you here all the time," Gwen began. "You've told me all about your wife and kids. You've showed me wonderful photos, and now you want to get busy with me."

"So?" Patrick shrugged.

"This isn't the Nick I know," Gwen declared.

"I'm not really Nick today."

"Oh, I see," Gwen nodded. "I've had some bullshit lines laid on me in the past but I've never had the split personality routine before."

"What are you talking about?"

"All these months you're the happy family man, but today you come on to me like a lowlife and when I shoot you down you say it's not really you." Gwen shook her head. "I guess when I see you next week you'll show me more family photos and have no memory of your outrageous behavior."

"I could never forget you, gorgeous," Patrick crooned.

"Well, I'm going to do my best to forget you, asshole," Gwen sneered. She began rolling her luggage to the front, but stopped in the middle of the car and turned back toward Patrick. "And do me a favor, whichever personality you happen to be, please don't ever speak to me again."

Patrick didn't move from his position at the rear of the car as the train made its Manhattan stops. He breathed a sigh of relief when the train pulled out of its only Brooklyn stop at Jay Street. Aside from some dirty looks from Gwen the flight attendant he had no further interactions with anyone in the car.

Patrick had never ridden the subway in Southern Queens and he was surprised when the blackness of the tunnel occupying his view changed to the landscape of residential Queens neighborhoods. As the train approached Howard Beach Patrick was struck by another odd sight. He had ridden on elevated subway trains before but shortly before the train approached the station it had descended to street level.

Melvin's voice filled the car. "This is Howard Beach - the last stop for this train. Transfer is available for the A train. Airport passengers may transfer to the JFK shuttle bus. Thank you for riding the Train to the Plane and have a great day."

Patrick remained glued to the rear door of the car until everyone but Melvin had detrained. He slowly walked forward scanning through the windows as he walked. Patrick wanted to make sure Gwen was nowhere in sight. The irate flight attendant was gone, but someone else was on the platform staring directly at him.

Most of the cops liked Sergeant Richie Addison. He wasn't the most personable man in the world but he was considered harmless. He was also considered odd by virtue of involuntary twitching of his head, neck, eyes, and mouth. Rumor had it that Richie developed these ticks after he contacted the electrified third rail while assisting an elderly man who had passed out and fallen to the tracks. Richie saved the man and received a medal. He also received the regular facial twitching which he would not acknowledge, and which got worse whenever he became excited or nervous.

Patrick was proud of himself when he noticed the sergeant's stripes and remembered his instructions to salute.

"How's it going, Montgomery?" Addison asked.

"Everything's cool with me," Patrick smiled. "How's it hanging with you?"

"What?" Addison's eyes and mouth twitched several times.

Patrick squinted as he focused on the sergeant's twitching face. "Holy cow," he blurted.

Addison's twitching increased as he attempted to ignore Patrick's exclamation. "I gotta get out of here. Let me give you a scratch before I go."

"Thanks, man," Patrick replied, "but I'm not itchy right now. I could have used you about a half hour ago. This bullet proof vest is a killer against the back of my neck."

Addison's head was now twitching like a piston. "Your memo book – I want to sign your memo book!"

"No problem, dude," Patrick said as he reached into his rear pants pocket.

Addison was still twitching as he inspected the memo book. "Your entries are not up to date so I left you a couple of lines to catch up before I signed."

"That's really nice of you," Patrick grinned as he took the memo book from the sergeant. Addison's head was now twitching violently to the right. "I hope I'm not out of line, dude, " Patrick remarked," but I gotta ask you, what's up with the twitching?"

Sergeant Addison didn't say a word. He turned and walked toward the station exit, twitching and shaking every step of the way. Patrick shrugged before pulling Nick's instruction sheet out of his pocket. He was scheduled to immediately return to Manhattan so he made an about face and boarded the train. The return trip was completely without incident, and as Patrick began his next run towards Howard Beach he was sorry he had never considered becoming a police officer. This job was so easy even he could do it.

Patrick checked his instruction sheet. When the train arrived at Howard Beach this time it would be time for him to take his meal break. Melvin's voice announced Howard Beach as the next stop. Once the passengers had filed out of the car, Patrick detrained to the platform to look for the token booth. The plan was proceeding like clockwork. He located the booth and waved at the clerk. Just as Nick predicted the clerk pulled the bolt on the small compartment giving Patrick access to the phone. He wedged the phone between his right shoulder and ear as he unfolded his instruction sheet and dialed the four-digit number for the District 1 desk officer.

Everyone from the Chief of the Department down to every sergeant at District 1 wished Police Officer Leon Manfred would retire. The twenty-two-year veteran was a classic "boss fighter" who could have written a book on the classic "us vs. them" police mentality. For Leon Manfred, however, his disdain went beyond the bosses on the job and the public. He despised most of the cops he worked with too. Despite his hate for everything about the job. Leon had no intention of retiring. Two years earlier, several weeks before his twentieth anniversary, he slipped and fell in the male police officer locker room. Leon claimed a back injury and cited the cause as being the negligence of the Transit Police porter in leaving the floor in a wet condition. Leon cancelled his retirement plans and spent the next two years trying to get a three quarters line of duty disability pension in lieu of the normal twenty-year service retirement. The difference in the two pensions was significant. The normal service retirement provided the retiree with a taxable pension of half his salary. The line of duty disability pension provided a tax-free pension of three quarters of the final salary. While Leon tried to convince the world that his back injury left him unable to perform the function of a full duty police officer, he remained on restricted duty while he fought the good fight for his disability pension.

Deputy Inspector Harding, the commanding officer of District 1, subscribed to the square pegs in square holes theory of management when he assigned Leon to be the steady assistant desk officer on day tours. As miserable as he was, Leon was competent, so he was able to handle the most important task of an A.D.O. – answering the phone. The bonus for the sergeants and lieutenants working as desk officers was that Leon's short and abrupt attitude on the phone meant that they rarely had to field any calls from the cops in the field. Leon would very quickly and gruffly exchange information with the caller and then hang up on them without any pleasantries.

It was during this time period that the Transit Police Department initiated a program of enhanced customer service that included phone courtesy. A department bulletin specified the manner in which department phones were to be answered:

Good (morning, afternoon, evening) Rank, Name, Command, How may I help you?

Deputy Inspector Harding was under no illusions that Leon Manfred was going to answer the phone according to the department protocol. He was happy that Leon answered the phone, even if it was in his own unique style. Leon answered the phone the same way every time, blurting out "District 1 – Manfred." The problem was that he spoke so quickly and his words were so slurred together that his greeting sounded like one word – Demented." Within a month of his assignment to the District 1 desk Leon Manfred had universally acquired the nickname of Demented Leon.

"District 1, Manfred."

The greeting was blurted so quickly and indistinctly that Patrick could not even hear the word "demented." It just sounded like unintelligible mumblings. "Stop the clock partner and take a breath."

"Who is this?" Manfred growled.

"That's better," Patrick said. "When you talk slower you don't sound like you have marbles in your mouth."

"Who the hell is this?" Manfred raised the level of his volume.

"Easy, dude," Patrick cautioned. "No need to shout. I can hear you."

Leon grit his teeth and whispered through them. "For the last time - who the hell is this?"

"This is Montgomery."

"What the hell is your problem, Montgomery?"

"No problem, dude. I'm just hanging out here at Howard Beach."

Leon's face had transitioned to three different shades of red. "You called to tell me you're hanging out at Howard Beach?"

"Oh yeah, " Patrick remembered. "It's lunch time. Anyplace good to eat over here?"

"Yeah," Leon replied. "There's a fried chicken place across the street. Go choke on a chicken bone." – click.

"Wow, that's quite an attitude," Patrick whispered to himself as he hung up the phone and closed the compartment door. He remembered his meal time instructions to go straight to the porter's room. He spun around to locate the room but was startled when he found himself face to face with another uniform. "Holy crap," he blurted, "you really snuck up on me."

"Sorry if I startled you," Lt. Beasley said.

"That's alright, dude, think nothing of it."

"Dude?" Beasley repeated. "Watch your professional demeanor, officer, and where is your salute?"

"Oh, sorry," Patrick said as he flipped a salute. "I didn't see any stripes, but I guess you're a big shot too. What are you, like a commodore or something like that?"

Beasley leaned in closer to get a whiff of Patrick's breath. "Are you drunk, Montgomery?"

"No, no," Patrick chuckled. "I was drunk last night, and normally I would be hung over right now. But surprisingly, I feel great."

"Don't be a smart ass just because you couldn't get off to leave for Disney," Beasley warned.

"Oh no, commodore," Patrick replied. "You got it all wrong. I'm not upset. I can't stand that Mickey Mouse crap anyway."

The muscles in Beasley's face were tight. "Call me commodore one more time and I'm gonna write you up."

Patrick held up both hands in front of him. "Sorry, no offense meant."

Beasley began to walk away, but after a few steps he wheeled around and pointed his finger at Patrick. "I came out here to tell you I felt sorry about having to disrupt your vacation, but now I'm glad your plans were ruined."

"I'm sorry I upset you," Patrick moaned. He reached into his pants pocket. "Here, do you want to autograph my book like that other guy?"

"This isn't over, Montgomery," Beasley warned as he exited the station.

Patrick grabbed the key ring off the gun belt as he approached the porter's room door. He shook his head as he opened the door. Maybe being a cop wasn't so great after all. There were too many kooks to deal with, and most of them were his bosses.

...

Allison Marcus was a rising star. The 42-year-old Manhattan mother of two had only entered politics two years earlier and had easily won a seat on the City Council as the representative for Manhattan's District 6.

Allison was a natural. She was bubbly and attractive with razor sharp wit and intelligence. And whether it was real or manufactured, she expressed a high degree of sincerity in her dealings with all, including the common people of the city.

There was so much to admire, but her raw honesty was what gained most admiration. When Allison spoke, her words spilled out slowly as if the truth needed to take its time. And in those words was a wonderful compassion, an awareness of the vulnerability of others, of the sort that is born of painful experience. When people told Allison about their problems and sorrows, they believed her when she said she knew how they felt. She was like a loving parent, supporting yet encouraging growth.

Everyone loved Allison Marcus, but the problem with universal love is who ends of becoming attracted. Kristof Borley was also 42-years old, but that's where the similarities with Allison ended. Borley lived with his mother in Brooklyn and worked as a US Post Office clerk in Manhattan inside Allison's 6th District

Borley possessed an unattractive personality to go along with his unkempt physical appearance. He had no friends and his co-workers had darkly voted him the postal worker most likely to go postal.

Besides his mother there was only one other person Kristof Borley cared for – Allison Marcus. When she was campaigning, Allison had spent many hours on the sidewalks of District 6, shaking hands and talking to the people. One of those hands she shook belonged to Borley. Allison spent a full ten minutes smiling and talking with Kristof, and when the conversation ended he was completely smitten. For an unstable personality like Borley, his infatuation with Allison would not be harmless. He quickly began following the FBI's five stages of stalking. Stage 1 began with Borley constantly calling Allison's office, trying to get her on the phone for a conversation. The more unsuccessful he was at getting her on the phone the more frustrated and upset he became. Kristof progressed to Stage 2 when he began hanging around outside Allison's office every day when he wasn't working. He never committed any overtly threatening or illegal acts, but he was beginning to be noticed by Allison and her staffers as he would wave and smile whenever she was entering or leaving her office. Stage 3 was entered when Borley was no longer smiling and saying hello anymore. Now, whenever he observed Allison entering or leaving her office he would shout, "Allison, you really should talk to me or you may be sorry." Borley had succeeded in getting Allison's attention, but she did not call the police because she did not want to overreact. Borley initiated Stage 4 with a series of letters to Allison, threating various forms of physical and sexual violence. Allison reported the threats to the police, but she did not connect the letters to the man standing outside her office. Stage 5 was actual violence towards the subject of the infatuation in the form of assault or abduction. As Patrick rode his last train of the day back to Manhattan he had no idea that Kristof Borley had just initiated Stage 5.

Allison Marcus had been taking care of some Saturday business at City Hall and was returning home for a restful Saturday afternoon. When she boarded the train at City Hall she did not notice the unkempt, angry-looking male who entered the same car and detrained with her at 57th Street. The stairway up to 57th Street was empty, but Allison paid no mind to the footsteps running up from behind her. Many people in the city are constantly in a hurry and scurrying from place to place. These running steps, however, came to an abrupt stop at the same time a large dirty hand reached around from behind and clasped tightly over her mouth. An arm grabbed her tightly around the waist and she could feel the hot breath on her ear as the man whispered. "Listen to me good, Allison. If you don't do exactly what I say, I'll kill you right now."

The man removed the grip from her waist to show that his left hand held a large steak knife. "Now, we're going back to the platform and onto a train, just like a happy couple walking arm in arm. If you scream or try to run, I'll slice your throat open on the spot."

Borley removed his hand from Allison's mouth, took her by the arm, draping a sweater over their arms to hide his knife. He then jerked her to the other direction and began leading her down the stairs. "Let's go," he ordered.

Patrick bounced off the train onto the 57th Street platform. His legs were fatigued from standing for far more time than he was used to, but there was suddenly renewed pep in his step. He had pulled off his charade as a cop. All he had to do now was walk back to District 1, turn in his radio, sign the log book and change out of the uniform. Then it would be straight to the Drunken Saint and a well-deserved afternoon and evening of serious drinking.

Patrick retraced his steps from early in the morning to the stairs at the south end of the platform. The stairs were empty when he began his ascent, but as he paused briefly to catch his breath at the landing he heard the clomping of multiple sets of feet coming down from the street. He looked up and observed a man and woman coming down the stairs. They appeared to be a couple walking arm in arm, but Patrick noted that they were a very strange looking couple. They were both White and appeared to be in their forties, but that is where any similarities ended. The woman was attractive, well-dressed and very polished looking, while the man was unkempt and greasy looking. Patrick also noted very different looks on their faces, both expressions equally strange. The male had a scowl of a person who was mad at the world while the woman had the glazed over eyes of a deer caught in headlights.

Patrick began climbing to the street and as he passed the couple he nodded at them. "Good afternoon, folks."

The man said nothing, but a second after they passed by Patrick thought he heard something strange. It sounded like the very soft whimpering of the word "help."

Patrick turned halfway up the stairs to face the couple who had now made it down to the landing. "Did you say something?" he inquired.

The woman stopped on the landing but the man apparently wanted to keep moving as he tugged on her right arm, causing the women's body to jerk violently. "Hey dude," Patrick called out, " take it easy. You're not playing football with the lady."

Patrick's admonishment was no more than a second old when the stair landing became a flurry of activity. First, it was no longer a faint whimper - it was the blood curdling scream of Allison Marcus pleading "Help me!"

The councilwoman's cry for assistance was followed immediately by the flash of a large steak knife as Borley backed up against the wall of the landing with his left arm wrapped tightly around Allison's chest and his right hand holding the large knife that was pressing against her throat.

"Stay back cop," Borley bellowed, "or I'll open her neck right now."

Patrick maintained his position half way up the stairs. He threw his arms out to the side. "What are you doing, dude? This is so unnecessary."

"I said to get out of here," Borley growled. "Get moving up those stairs or I'll kill her right now."

While the drama was unfolding a couple of people began coming up the stairs from the platform and two more started coming down the stairs from the street. When they observed the scene on the landing they quickly reversed course and made a dash for the nearest pay phones to call 911.

Perhaps Patrick didn't know enough about these situations to realize what danger Allison was in. He was more annoyed with what was taking place, and he let Borley know it as he took a couple of steps down the stairs. "You're way out of line, dude. You really need to get a grip on all this hostility."

"Shut up!" Borley screamed. "I'll slice you into pieces."

"See what I mean. That's a lot of pent of hostility," Patrick said as he inched closer.

"I'm warning you - shut up!" Borley screamed.

Patrick continued to advance down the stairs. "I used to keep in my hostility too," he said. "There a good book I will recommend for you, and meditation works wonders also."

Patrick stepped onto the landing as Borley let out an animal-like wail. It was unclear whether Allison broke free of his grasp or whether he threw her aside. What was clear, however, was that he was charging at Patrick with the knife at the ready. Borley continued screaming as he raised the knife above his head and stabbed down. Patrick threw up his left arm and blocked the attack before wrapping his armed around Borley and pushing him up against the wall. The knife flew out of Borley's hands as both the combatants fell to the landing floor.

Sirens were increasing in intensity as Patrick tried to keep control of his struggling adversary. Suddenly, it seemed like there were at least ten sets of hands all around, grabbing Borley and pulling him away. Patrick rolled away and got to his feet. An NYPD sergeant was the first person he saw. "Oh yeah, that's right," Patrick said as he tried to catch his breath. "You're one of those guys I have to salute."

The sergeant placed his hand on Patrick's shoulder. "I'm not sure what you're talking about, but are you okay?"

"Yeah, yeah," Patrick huffed. "I'll live, but what was up with that dude? He was way out of line."

"I guess you could say that," the sergeant replied as he observed Patrick to make sure his brain hadn't been rattled in the struggle.

The word of the abduction and rescue of Councilwoman Marcus was spreading quickly. Sergeant Ron Phillips, from District 1 arrived on the scene with a District 1 cop. "Oh, no," Patrick moaned at the sight of the sergeant, "another guy with stripes, " he said as he flipped a quick salute. "A cop could hurt his arm with all this saluting that has to be done."

Sergeant Phillips ignored the comment and got right to his business. "Officer Lincoln will take charge of your prisoner and process the arrest. I have been directed to transport you immediately to the Chief of Patrol's office."

"How long is this gonna take?" Patrick asked.

"What?" the sergeant did not understand the response.

"This has been a long day already and I'm supposed to meet some people at the bar in a couple of hours, so is this visit to that guy's office really necessary?"

"Are you feeling okay. Montgomery?" Phillips asked.

"Yeah, I'm sorry," Patrick said. "Let's get going. The sooner we get this over with the sooner I can get to the bar."

Sergeant Phillips glanced at Officer Lincoln and mouthed the word "Wow," as he rolled his eyes.

The media was already beginning to assemble at 370 Jay Street, the Brooklyn headquarters of the Transit Police Department. Police Officer Herby Dowdle, Chief Reed's administrative assistant and whipping boy was waiting on the sidewalk when the Transit Police patrol car pulled up to the curb. Sgt. Phillips turned toward the back seat. "Good luck, Montgomery."

Patrick exited the back seat and made a quick stop at the front seat passenger window. "Thanks for the lift, pal," he smiled.

Herby Dowdle grabbed Patrick by the arm. "Come on, hurry – the Chief is waiting for you."

As Patrick and Herby disappeared into the Jay Street lobby, Sgt. Phillips turned towards his driver and shook his head. "It's a good thing he's a hero because there is something definitely wrong with that guy."

Herby was talking at a mile a minute as they rode the elevator up one floor. "The Chief will begin the press conference by making some opening comments - then Councilwoman Marcus will speak. You will stand there quietly until it's question time. Don't say too much, just answer their questions as succinctly as possible."

"Whoa," Patrick said as the elevator door opened. "Slow down, man. Why so frantic? I didn't understand a word you said."

Herby shook his head and rolled his eyes as he opened the door to the Chief of Patrol's office. Chief Reed was coming out of his bathroom after changing into full dress uniform. Herby provided the introduction. "This is officer Montgomery, Chief."

"Yeah, yeah," Reed grumbled. "Nice to meet you, hero. Now let's get over to the conference room so we can get this press conference going."

Patrick was focused on Reed's uniform, particularly the three gold stars on each shoulder and the gold braid on his hat. "Wow, look at all that gold," Patrick exclaimed. "You must be the top banana here."

"The top what?" Reed asked.

"And look at the size of you," Patrick continued. "You're like Incredible Hulk size."

Herby grabbed Patrick by the arm. "Are you insane?" he whispered.

Lieutenant Beasley burst into the Chief's office, inadvertently saving Patrick from the Chief's wrath.

"It seems like every time I see you Beasley," Reed said, "you're late for something. You must want me to break out my flyswatter again.

"Sorry Chief," Beasley sniveled, "but I rushed over here as soon as I was notified."

Reed held his huge hand up in a stop sign. "Shut up and let's get this show on the road." He pointed a menacing finger at Beasley. "The hero will accompany me to the front of the conference room. You will stay in the back of the room."

The cameras clicked as Chief Reed entered the conference room and walked directly to the wood podium with the Transit Police logo attached. As directed, Lt. Beasley slunk to the back of the room behind the reporters while Patrick stood to the side of the podium next to Councilwoman Marcus.

As Reed made some opening remarks, Allison leaned over and whispered into Patrick's ear. "You're my hero."

Patrick could feel his face blushing. "I'm not like Batman, or anyone like that. I'm just glad I was there to help."

"And I'm glad you were there too," Allison smiled before turning to listen to Chief Reed.

"Once again, a member of the Transit Police Department has distinguished himself in a heroic manner," Reed said. "And this time, the officer was from a unit not normally associated with enforcement activities. Officer Nick Montgomery is a member of the Train to the Plane Unit, and is normally assigned to look out for the safety of the passengers riding the Train to the Plane. Earlier today, Officer Montgomery was finishing up his last assigned train run at the 57th Street station when he encountered a male perpetrator attempting to abduct City Councilwoman Allison Marcus at knifepoint. Officer Montgomery displayed the highest levels of police professionalism in taking the perpetrator into custody with no injuries occurring to Councilwoman Marcus, himself, or the perpetrator. That is how a professional police officer conducts business." Reed took a deep breath and cleared his throat. "Now, we'll be happy to answer any questions."

The first few questions were for Allison where she had the opportunity to express how lucky she was and how fortunate she felt that officer Montgomery was in the area. She also used to opportunity to talk about the importance of properly funding the police as well as mental health programs.

Finally, a female reporter switched interview subjects. "Officer Montgomery, I understand you were able to arrest the knife wielding man without even taking your gun out of its holster. Could you run us through how the arrest occurred?"

"Sure," Patrick replied. "I was pretty sure something bogus was going on when I passed those two on the stairs. When I saw the knife, I was thinking about pulling out my gun and plugging the guy, but I'm not sure how to take that damn lock off the holster."

There was a stunned silence in the room, giving Chief Reed a chance to jump in. "I think what the officer is saying is that after his initial assessment of the situation of the incident he believed he did not need to draw his weapon."

Patrick nodded and smiled. "That's right. It's like the big guy says. I realized I didn't need to plug anyone."

A male reporter jumped in. "Did you at least handcuff him during the struggle?"

Patrick stroked his chin. "You know, I was thinking about that, but I was fooling around with those handcuffs during my lunch break, and those things are complicated."

Chief Reed placed his huge arm around Patrick's shoulder and smiled at the reporters. "I think we're done here. I'm sure Councilwoman Marcus will be glad to answer any additional questions."

With that, George Reed dragged Patrick out of the conference room with more force than Kristof Borley had used on Allison Marcus.

He did not release Patrick until he tossed him into the chair in front of his huge oak desk. "Now," he huffed, "I'm only gonna ask this once. Who they hell are you?"

Patrick shrugged and tried to smile. "Well, you see, Mr. Big, it's a long story."

...

Saturday afternoon, a well-tanned, well-rested Nick Montgomery tossed several pieces of luggage on the living room floor and turned to make a second trip to the car. His progress was suspended, however, by the sight of the flashing red light on the phone next to the dining room table. The first message caused him to lose every ounce of good feeling he had built up over the last week.

"Montgomery," the voice growled, "this is Chief Reed. Monday, be in my office at 9 a. m. sharp, and don't give me any crap about being your day off. Your day off is cancelled." BEEP.

Nick was out the door and into his car before his wife had a chance to question him. The Drunken Saint was dark and empty, except for three drunks spread out at the bar. Thankfully for Nick, one of the drunks was Patrick.

"What the hell happened?" Nick growled.

"Hey, big brother," Patrick beamed. "Welcome home. How was Goofy and Pluto?"

"You're the only thing goofy around here," Nick snapped. "What the hell happened?"

"What are you talking about?"

"Why do I have a phone message waiting for me from a very angry Chief ordering me into his office on Monday morning."

"Oh, that," Patrick chuckled. "Don't lose any sleep over that. I explained everything to the Incredible Hulk and we ended up seeing eye to eye."

"You explained everything?" Nick was beginning to feel weak in the knees. "You mean he knows who you are?"

"Yeah, I had to come clean. That big gorilla was ready to swat me with some big-ass fly swatter, so I had to spill the beans."

"You spilled the beans," Nick sighed as he slumped onto a stool.

"Don't look so forlorn, Nicky. Me and the big cheese parted as good friends."

"Good friends – that's great," Nick mumbled as he slowly made his way to the door.

...

At 8:50 a.m. on Monday morning Herby Dowdle escorted Nick into Chief Reed's office and sat him in a chair in front of the Chief's desk. The Chief was not present, but the office was not empty. Sitting in a second chair in front of the desk was Lt. Beasley.

"The Chief will be along momentarily," Herby said. "Good luck," he whispered as he stepped out of the office.

"Well, Montgomery," Beasley snapped, "you've really done it. You just couldn't accept that you couldn't get the day off so you had to pull a stunt that may very well cost you your job and your pension."

Nick sat silently staring straight ahead.

Beasley shook his head. "I hope you're satisfied with all the trouble you caused."

The office door opened and Chief Reed came stomping in. He did not move behind his desk but instead his immense form stood hovering over Nick. "I'm gonna make this really quick," Reed began. "First of all, I know exactly what you did."

Beasley decided to join in. "I was just telling him how outrageous..."

"Shut up!" Reed bellowed. "If I want your input I'll ask for it." His glare retuned to Nick. "With this bizarre stunt you orchestrated you should be going to jail. My God, just the fact that you gave that lunatic brother of yours your gun should be enough to land you in a jail cell." Reed took a deep breath and sighed. "But there is another consideration. We had the ultimate feel good story where a hero transit cop saved a city councilwoman from being abducted by a stalker. I don't want to ruin the good PR we got out of this so there's only one thing I can do." Reed reached into his jacket pocket and slammed something into Nick's hand. It was a distinguished duty medal. "I really want to jam that medal up your ass. Now be a good hero and take your God damn medal and get the hell out of my sight before I change my mind."

"Yes, sir," Nick blurted as he scurried for the door.

Beasley attempted to follow Nick out but was stopped by a howling voice. "Where do you think you're going? Get the hell back here."

When Beasley had slumped back into the chair Reed unloaded. "What kind of an imbecile are you? How could you allow one of your cops to use his twin brother in his place?"

"But Chief," Beasley pled, "how could I..."

"Shut up!" Reed cut him off. "And don't think I don't realize that you are the root cause of this entire debacle. You wouldn't give the man one day off so he could leave on his family vacation. What kind of moron are you?"

"That excusal would have put me above the quota." Beasley said.

"Quota?" Reed shouted. "You know something, Lieutenant. I'm below my quota in thrashing asshole lieutenants." He scanned his desktop. "Where the hell is that thing? It's never available when I need it."

The office door swung open and Herby Dowdle stuck his torso though the door. "Are you looking for this, Chief?" he asked as he held up the large Transit Police flyswatter.

"I sure am," Reed said as he grabbed the flyswatter from his lackie. "I knew there was a reason I keep you around here."

"Thank you, Chief." Herby smiled. "That's very nice of you to say."

Herby closed the door and continued to his desk. The smile remained on his face as he heard the swishing and smacking sounds coming from inside the Chief's office.

...

Doug could hardly restrain his delight. Of course, Lt. Beasley wanted to bury this embarrassing story deep in the incident binder, but how could he argue with the inclusion of the tale of a transit police hero in the request for the unit citation. Doug's two fingers were back at work. He was really beginning to enjoy this assignment he had initially hated.

CHAPTER 8: The Story of Police Officer Larry Bowman

Larry Bowman was typical of most of the cops who made up the Train to the Plane Unit. The 40-year-old fifteen-year veteran didn't want to do anything more than ride out his last five years so he could retire and move to Florida. He certainly had no interest in performing police work. Two years earlier Larry had found a safe haven on the Train to the Plane. He worked steady 4 p.m. to 12 a.m. and as a bonus he usually earned an hour overtime most tours because the final train of the night usually pulled into 57th Street around 1 a.m..

Larry not only complied with Lt. Beasley's edict never to get off the train – he celebrated it. The last thing in the world Larry wanted was to get involved with an incident that could involve police work. To that end, Larry had set up routines for himself that would make it as least likely as possible that he would ever walk into a situation requiring him to take action.

When Train to the Plane cops reported on duty at District 1 they had to sign in the log book and sign out a radio. Some took care of these duties immediately after entering the district before going to the locker room to change into uniform. Other cops waited until they were in full uniform before signing in and obtaining a radio.

Larry always signed the log book and picked up a radio as soon as he entered the district. He then proceeded to the locker room, but he did not change into uniform. Larry would loiter at his locker for a few minutes before nonchalantly departing the command without being in uniform. Larry did this to eliminate the prime time when he could be forced into a police action. District 1 was at Columbus Circle, two very long blocks from where the Train to the Plane originated at the 57th Street station. A cop making that walk in uniform was fair game for any member of the public seeking assistance, so Larry was not in uniform when he made the walk. During the winter months it was easy. Larry simply wore a heavy winter coat over his uniform so no one could recognize him as a cop. During warm weather Larry always wore his uniform pants and shoes, but he carried the remainder of his uniform items in a bag. After making the incognito walk to 57th Street in civilian attire, Larry would key his way into one of the locked conductor's cabs on the Train to the Plane and change into uniform.

Larry also had a system to stay below the radar at Howard Beach, the terminal station for the train. Larry always brought his lunch with him because he never wanted to leave the station and risk getting involved in the street. His meal period was always 9:30 p. m., an assignment Larry loved. When his meal was over at 10:30 he only had one more train run back to 57th Street and that train usually departed Howard beach at 11:30. From 10:30 to 11:30 Larry was supposed to patrol the Howard Beach station, but he remained squirreled away in the locked porter's room until it was time for the train to depart.

Once Larry was inside that porter's room he would never come out until it was time for him to leave on the train. He didn't even have to worry about a porter wanting access to the room because Nat Coleman, the porter assigned to Howard Beach worked from 6 a.m. to 2 p.m..

Larry took care of all his business inside that porter's room, and taking care of his business is what ultimately got him in trouble. Once Larry was inside the room he would wolf down his sandwich before settling into the chair as best as he could for a nap. At about 11:00 Larry would begin to stir. He usually had one more bit of business to take care of before heading off to the train.

Larry's digestive system had developed a new routine since he began taking a new blood pressure medication. Since beginning the medication Larry had to evacuate around the time he was getting ready to leave the porter's room. In other words, he had to take a dump. The employee bathroom was on the other side of the station, a walk that Larry found unacceptable due to the high risk of running into a member of the public looking for a police officer. If he was unwilling to risk the walk to the bathroom, this seemed like a serious conundrum – but not for Larry. Larry believed the best solutions were usually the simplest ones, and the simplest solution for Larry was to drop his pants and take care of his business inside a metal bucket that was kept inside the porter's room.

Larry didn't think or didn't care about the scene at 6 a.m. the next morning when Nat Coleman entered the porter's room. Nat was livid when he discovered the prize left for him inside the bucket, but he did his job and disposed of the gift and cleaned the bucket. He did this for two weeks until he couldn't stand it anymore. Nat reported the condition to his superintendent who in turn reported it to the Transit Police. Eventually, the complaint reached District 23, the Transit Police District that covered the Howard Beach station. The commanding officer of District 23 assigned the plainclothes anti-crime unit to investigate the condition, which instantly became known as the case of the "Mad Shitter."

The information that the anti-crime unit had to work with was that when Nat Coleman departed work at 2 p.m. every day, the room was fine, but upon returning the next day at 6 a.m. he would find that a deposit had been made. It did not take a brain surgeon to deduce that the Mad Shitter was striking sometime after 2 p.m. but before 6. a.m.

Teddy Lyons and Pete Van Horn were the anti-crime cops assigned to the case. Teddy told anti-crime sergeant Fred Barnes that he wanted to re-interview Nat Coleman to attempt to narrow the time frame of when the acts were being committed. When Barnes asked how he was going to narrow the time frame Teddy said he was going to ask Nat what the turds looked like when he discovered them. Teddy theorized that if the turds were hot and steaming then the acts were taking place shortly before 6 a.m..

Sergeant Barnes directed Teddy to forget his "steam" theory and to just work 4 p.m. to 12 a.m. to try to catch the perpetrator. The first two nights of the stakeout went by without incident. In retrospect, this was to be expected because these first two days were Larry's regular days off. Day three of the operation appeared to be another big bowl of nothing. The only people who entered the room while Teddy and Pete were secreted on the station were two Train to the Plane cops on their meal periods.

Teddy and Pete were flabbergasted when they arrived at District 23 the next day to find an irate Sergeant Barnes waiting for them.

"Well?" Barnes snarled.

"Well, what?" Teddy replied.

"The porter from Howard Beach called this morning. He said there was a big fresh turd waiting for him when he arrived this morning."

"Then it has to be happening after we leave at midnight," Teddy theorized. "The only people who accessed the room while we were there were a couple of Train to the Plane cops."

"Then start working midnights," Barnes ordered. "I want to be done with this shitty case."

"You got it sarge," Teddy called out as Barnes walked away.

"Hey Teddy," Pete said, "It's good that we have one more night on 4 to 12's."

"Why?"

"Because there is one thing we never did."

"What didn't we do?" Teddy asked.

"We never checked the room before we left."

Teddy threw his arms out to the side. "But no one entered the room – except for the cops."

"You see where I'm going," Pete nodded.

"Oh, no!" Teddy shook his head. "You don't think the cops could..."

"Who knows?" Pete shrugged. "We'll soon find out."

At 5:30 p.m. Officer Tony Mara left the porter's room and locked the padlock on the door. Two minutes later Teddy and Pete opened the lock and threw the door open. The room was clean. They settled back into their observation point and waited. At 9:30 Larry Bowman keyed his way into the room. There was no further activity until Larry left the room at 11:30, locked the door and hustled to the platform to catch his train.

"This was a waste of time," Teddy yawned.

"Okay, let's go check the room and get ready for midnights," Pete said.

Pete had the key to the room, and when he opened the lock and threw open the door, the smell hit him like a freight train. "Oh, my God!" he groaned.

Teddy shook his head. "I don't believe it. The Train to the Plane cop is the Mad Shitter."

When Larry Bowman arrived at District 1 the next afternoon, he was unable to perform his quick departure from the command after signing in and picking up a radio. He had a welcoming committee waiting for him. The commanding officer of District 1 wanted nothing to do with it, since it didn't involve one of his cops, but he gladly allowed his office to be used for the interview. Lt. Beasley, Inspector Harrington, the Commanding Officer of Citywide Patrol Services, Lt. Malcolm from the Employees Assistance Unit, and Dr. Billings, a psychiatrist from the Employee Counseling Unit were jammed into the small office when Larry wedged his way in.

Lt. Beasley began the interview as only he could. "Officer Bowman, it's been alleged that you have been defecating in the porter's room at Howard Beach. Do you deny it?"

"No," Larry shrugged.

"Why are you doing it?" Dr. Billings asked.

"Because I have to go," Larry replied.

"What I meant," Dr. Billings continued, "is why don't you go to the bathroom?"

Larry had to think for a moment. He didn't want to admit that he was looking to avoid having to take a police action at all costs. He cleared his throat. "Well, my stomach gets kind of jumpy at that time of night, and it's a long walk to the bathroom on the station. If I try to make it to the bathroom I will probably soil my uniform pants on the way."

"So, you believed your best option was to shit in the porter's room?" Inspector Harrington asked.

"Yes sir," Larry nodded. "I was very neat about it too. I always used the bucket. I never went on the floor."

Harrington rolled his eyes. "That was very considerate of you," he said.

"Thank you," Larry nodded, completely missing the Inspector's sarcasm.

"Okay," Beasley said, "the officer has admitted his guilt. Now it's just a matter of determining whether he is nuts or not."

"That's not how I would care to characterize it," Dr. Billings cautioned.

"Officer Bowman," Inspector Harrington said, "You are going to be transported to Jay Street so that Dr. Billings can perform a complete evaluation of you. After I receive his report, you will be notified of the disposition of this case. Until that time, I am suspending you from duty."

"I'm being suspended because I took a dump?" Larry groaned.

"Give me your shield and gun, officer," Beasley directed.

It took less than 24-hours for Dr. Billings to report that Larry's unique bathroom habits had nothing to do with any psychological disorder. With no mental issues to deal with, Inspector Harrington returned Larry to full duty, but transferred him to District 11 in the Bronx, where he was assigned to work steady midnights. Larry's digestive system suffered as a result of the transfer and change of hours. Suddenly, there were several wild reports originating from the motormen of trains in the Bronx. In each of these reports, the train operators reported that as they were pulling out of a station, the light from the train allowed them to see some activity on the catwalk just inside the tunnel. The motormen were never certain of their observations, but they all said it looked like a person on the catwalk squatting with their pants down, and that the person appeared to be wearing a police uniform.

Larry Bowman had learned a valuable lesson about the porter's room. Still, when you have to go, you have to go!

...

Doug Collins was elated after reading the report regarding the Larry bowman incident. He began typing and envisioning Beasley's face when he discovered that the case of the Mad Shitter had been included in the request for the unit citation.

CHAPTER 9: The Story of Police Officer Sal Carbone

Sal Carbone had a problem. In reality, he had two problems – his knees. The 43-year old had been diagnosed with osteoarthritis in both knees. Osteoarthritis is the most common form of arthritis and involves the degenerative, wear and tear type of arthritis that occurs most in people over fifty years of age. The cartilage in the knee gradually wears away, becoming frayed and rough, and the protective space between the bones decreases. This results in bone rubbing on bone, and produces painful bone spurs. Sal had reached the point where he was experiencing multiple symptoms. His knees were regularly stiff and swollen, and it was difficult for him to bend and straighten the knees. The pain varied in intensity, and Sal found it most unbearable in the morning and after he had been sitting for an extended period. Physical activity was also problematic, and Sal reached a point where he had virtually eliminated activities that aggravated his condition, such as impact activities like walking, jogging, and tennis. The doctor said that getting rid of the fifty pounds of excess weight he was carrying around would be an excellent way for Sal to reduce the stress on his knees, but Sal loved to eat too much to make such a drastic change to his lifestyle.

Sal tried the full menu of non-surgical treatments. He went to physical therapy and wore special shock absorbing shoes. Sal also tried several over the counter and prescribed medications as well as a series of cortisone injections. At the end of the day Sal knew he had run out of non-surgical treatments. The problem he faced was that he did not want to undergo any surgeries, and there was only so much he could do to limit the time he would have to stand. Sal was a transit police officer, a police officer required to stand for the majority of his shift.

With 17-years on the job Sal only had three more years to make it to twenty and a full retirement pension. But with the way his knees felt three years may well have been a hundred. Since his knee condition was not a line of duty injury, Sal's only alternative if he could not make it the three years would be to take an ordinary medical disability pension, which would result in a pension significantly less than the amount he would receive for the normal twenty-year retirement.

As bad as they were, Sal's aching knees never stopped him from tossing back beers several times a week at the Blue Brigade, a cop bar in Queens.

The stool next to Sal rocked slightly under the weight of a new occupant. "What's wrong, Sally Boy?" Roy Mathias asked. "You look like you just found out the pizza joint next door went out of business."

"Very funny, Roy," Sal sighed. "My God damn knees are killing me. I don't know how much longer I can take it."

Roy rolled his eyes. "You know, losing a few pounds might help."

Sal waved his right hand dismissively while he took a big sip of beer with his left hand. "Spare me the diet lecture," he said as he plopped the bottle down on the bar.

"I don't know how many times I've told you," Roy shrugged. "You have to avoid standing as much as you can."

"That's easy for you to say," Sal scoffed. "You work in a precinct and drive around all day sitting in an NYPD patrol car."

Roy took a sip of beer before letting out a large chuckle. "Hey, that Train to the Plane Unit you're in isn't exactly a powder keg of police activity, is it?"

"No, it's not," Sal agreed, "but I have to stand on that train for almost the entire tour." He shook his head and looked down at his beer. "I'm telling you, Roy, I'm not gonna make it to twenty. They're gonna end up putting me out on an ordinary medical."

Roy placed his arm on Sal's shoulder. "Chin up, my friend. There is a solution to everything."

"Cut the bullshit," Sal scoffed.

"Do you know what I wanted to be when I was a kid?" Roy asked.

"A cop?" Sal snickered.

"A cop was the last thing I wanted to be," Roy replied. "For as long as I can remember I wanted to be a magician."

"You're kidding?"

Roy shook his head. "No, I'm serious. When I was five years old my dad took me to a magic show where the magician made a lady disappear into thin air. From that moment I was hooked. I lived and breathed magic. I read every book I could get my hands on and almost every Christmas and birthday present I received was magic-related."

"I'm sure you will magically make a point soon," Sal remarked.

"Patience," Roy shot back. "By the time I graduated high school I had acquired enough magic supplies and props to rival most professional magicians. I even began getting some work putting on magic shows in some East Village coffee houses."

"So, what happened?" Sal asked.

"I could never break through to the next level," Roy said. "My dad said he was going to do a trick to make my nose turn red if I didn't get a real job – so here I am."

"That was a great story," Sal said, "but I'm still waiting for the point."

Roy turned on the stool to face Sal. "Listen, magic is all about illusion. It makes a person not able to see what is right in front of them. It's all about props, diversions and misdirection. Magic is about creating the illusion that the impossible is actually possible. I still get some gigs once in a while in low-end comedy clubs that are looking for a change of pace from their usual stand-up comedians. When I go on stage, I don't hold up a saw and say, 'ladies and gentlemen, I would love to saw this young lady in half, but obviously it is impossible.'" Roy shook his head. "No, I create the illusion that I sawed her in half. I create the illusion that I made her disappear. I create the illusion that I levitated her."

"I'm still waiting for the point," Sal grinned.

Roy pointed his finger at Sal. "The point is that you don't have to stand all day while you're riding that train. We just have to create the illusion that you're standing."

"I appreciate you trying to help," Sal responded, "but that sounds insane."

"Come on, Sally," Roy urged. "This conversation has got my magical juices flowing. An idea has already popped into my head if you'll let me help you."

Sal sighed and shrugged. "I guess I have nothing to lose. What do you need?"

"I need to get on the type of train you ride every day to see if the logistics will work."

"That's easy," Sal replied. "The Train to the Plane, like most of the other IND lines uses R44 cars. There's always layup trains at 57th Street. I can key my way onto a layup train and you can take as much time as you need working your magic."

"I'm RDO Sunday and Monday," Roy said.

"Same here," Sal added.

"How about we do this Sunday morning," Roy suggested.

"That works," Sal agreed. "They'll be the most layup trains sitting there on Sunday morning anyway."

"Great," Roy declared, "we have a date. I only need you to bring one thing."

"What?"

"A stool that when you sit on it your head will be at the same height as if you were standing."

"I guess I can rig something up," Sal said, "but I don't know what it will accomplish."

"You'll see, my friend," Roy said. "And now, I have to get out of here."

"Aren't you supposed to say abracadabra, or something," Sal smiled.

"Shut up and watch me make my beer disappear," Roy said as he grabbed his bottle.

•••

The R-44 subway car was put into service in 1972. They were the first 75-foot length cars and featured full width operator cabs in each car. Sal and Roy had made a wise choice of days to work on their scheme because on Sunday morning the 57th Street station, which was usually bustling with activity, was almost deserted. Additionally, there were several layup trains on the station for them to choose from.

Sal grimaced in discomfort as he carried his stool down the stairs to the platform. Roy carried a much heavier load in the two large duffel bags, but he navigated the trip to the platform with much less effort.

Sal took a few deep breaths as he set his stool on the platform and pulled a key ring out of his pocket that housed at least thirty keys. He did not have to search through the keys because the train key was substantially longer and thicker than all the other keys. He inserted the key into the slot at the top of the train car door and turned. One of the double doors slid open allowing Sal and Roy to bring their gear into the car.

Sal inserted the key in a similar slot on the inside of the car. "Okay," he said as the door slid closed. "Now, you can work your magic undisturbed."

Roy looked around the car as he scratched his chin. "So, you stay in a car exactly like this when you ride your train, right?"

"That's correct," Sal nodded.

"Does it matter where you stay in the car?" Roy asked.

"Not at all," Sal shrugged. "I can stay wherever I want in the car, but the problem is that I have to stand."

"Well, that's the illusion we are going to create," Roy smiled. "The illusion that you are standing."

"I don't know how you're gonna do that," Sal replied, "but good luck."

Roy pointed to the operator's cab at the rear of the car. "Do you have access to that cab?"

"Sure," Roy replied. "It opens with the same train key."

"And you could stand right in front of that door for your entire train run if you wanted to?" Roy asked.

"I could," Sal nodded, "but standing in one place only makes the pain worse."

"Who said anything about standing?" Roy grinned.

"What?"

"Go set your stool up in front of the cab door," Roy directed, "and I'll show you what I mean."

Sal placed the stool in front of the door and turned to see Roy pulling a set of life size legs out of one of his bags.

"What the hell," Sal blurted.

Sal held up the legs with one hand. "They are a very light weight rubber-like material – very light, flexible, and easy to work with. They are an essential element in my saw the person in half trick." He handed the legs to Sal and returned to his second bag. "This one is the key to the illusion," he crooned as he pulled the object out of the bag.

Sal tilted his head slightly and squinted as he tried to figure out exactly what was being displayed. As best as he could see it looked like the mold of the torso of a man, complete with arms and hands, but only the front half. It looked like the hollow mold had been split into two pieces and the back half had been removed.

"Isn't it great?" Roy beamed.

"As soon as you let me know what you're gonna do with it I'll let you know."

"The concept is simple." Roy began. "Once you're comfortable with the basic concept we can refine it."

"Go ahead, Merlin," Sal sighed.

"Hop up on your stool," Roy directed. "Now, rest your legs on the horizontal support pieces on the stool or move them to the side – whichever is a more comfortable position for you."

"Okay," Sal said as he raised his feet up onto the wooden supports.

"Now we'll put these right in front of you," Roy said and he stood the legs directly in front of the stool. "Now, for the most important part," he said as he moved forward with the torso piece. "It's like putting on a suit of armor, only much lighter. Grab onto the two handles on the inside and put your head into the cutout neck area."

Roy took two steps back to admire his creation. "It's perfect," he declared.

"I feel ridiculous," Sal groaned. "This will never work."

"Let me sit there," Roy suggested, "and you take a look."

Two minutes later Sal stood in the middle of the car, silently studying the scene before him.

"You can't fully appreciate how lifelike this looks because you're seeing the white color of the molds," Roy said. "When your uniform is over them no one will be able to tell the difference." Roy smiled. "Of course, we'll have to add some padding under your shirt."

"Watch it!" Sal cautioned.

"And look at this feature," Roy said. Suddenly, the right arm attached to the torso jumped up two feet as it was greeting someone.

"How did you do that?" Sal asked

"From the handles on the torso." Roy replied. "Squeeze the right one and the right arm moves. Squeeze the left one and the left arm moves. The movement is very realistic, isn't it?

"It is," Sal admitted.

"The moving arms are a very important feature when I'm sawing someone in half. The audience is convinced the subject is still inside the box because the arms are moving. In my act, I have a way of making the feet move too, but we don't need to do that for our purposes."

"Is there anything else we need to do?" Sal asked.

"There's only one more factor that could make this a waste of time." Roy said.

"Oh, no," Sal moaned, "here it comes."

"Are you changing trains during your shift or do you stay on the same train."

"For my assignment," Sal replied. "I stay on the same train for the entire shift."

"Perfect!" Roy exclaimed. "If you were changing trains during the shift it would be completely impractical to think that you would be dragging your stool and props on and off the train." Roy took a deep breath. "One final hurdle. Is there anywhere near the place you get on the train at the start of your shift where you could stash the props?"

"Yeah," Sal replied, "there's a signal room directly across from the platform where I pick up my train."

Roy clapped his hands. "That's it then – we're set. When you arrive for your shift, you go into the signal room, bring your props onto the train and set yourself up on the stool." A wide grin appeared on Roy's face. "Then all you have to do is sit there and enjoy the ride. If you have to leave the train when you go to meal, just stash all the stuff in the cab until you get back."

Sal worked out a few more details himself before returning to work Tuesday morning. He would bring an extra uniform shirt and pants with him so that he could leave the legs and torso dressed. He would also bring an old gun belt he still had as well as a toy gun his son had as a kid. The toy looked something like a real revolver – at least enough for Sal's purposes. The final detail would require Sal to bring his "Dupe."

Most cops buy a duplicate shield, which looks like the real shield but is only slightly smaller. The reason to have a dupe is so the real shield can be stored in a safe location while the dupe is carried to work and worn on the uniform. If the dupe is lost, the cop simply had to go out and buy another one. If the real shield was lost, there was a ton of paperwork and serious disciplinary consequences. Sal would wear the real shield on his uniform and place his dupe on the shirt covering the torso prop."

When Tuesday morning rolled around Sal was gaining more and more confidence that this wild scheme could actually work. He arrived at 57th Street much earlier than usual so he could go to the signal room, retrieve his stool and props and dress the legs and torso on the train before anyone else arrived.

When he had completed dressing his alter-ego, Sal hopped up on the stool, grabbed the torso's handles and moved his head into position. He was relieved to find that the position was comfortable, and he reckoned he could stay in the same seated position on the stool all day without any problem.

Sal detected some activity on the platform. His first test was about to begin. Marty Gibbons and Joe Brown entered the car. Marty was the motorman for the train and Joe was the conductor.

Marty called out, "Good morning, Sal," before disappearing into his operator's cab.

"Morning, Sal," Joe said. "You're here bright and early."

"Yeah," Sal replied. "I couldn't sleep last night so I woke up earlier than I normally do."

Joe had a few more comments but Sal wasn't listening. He was too ecstatic to pay attention. This ridiculous scheme was actually working. Marty and Joe had looked right at him and hadn't noticed anything out of the ordinary. Maybe he could ride out his last three years after all.

The Train to the Plane departed Manhattan and raced under the river toward Brooklyn. Sal was both elated and astonished. Roy really was a magician. The car full of passengers was under the illusion that a stoic police officer was standing tall watching over them from the rear of the car. Little did they know that the cop with the bum knees was actually resting on a stool. Just for effect, every few minutes Sal would squeeze one of the handles causing his arm to raise up momentarily.

When the train pulled into the Jay Street station his spirits had soared to heights he had not seen in years. Those spirits went into a complete nose dive, however, as soon as the door opened. Only one passenger boarded the train, but that one passenger caused Sal to become light headed to the point that he feared he may pass out.

Lt. Beasley made a quick scan of the car before striding directly towards Sal. He began addressing the stationery officer as he approached. "Hello Carbone. I just came out of a meeting at the Chief's officer, so I figured I'd come down here and pay you a visit."

"That's good sir," Sal nodded as sweat built up on his forehead.

A frown had taken possession of Beasley's face. "What's wrong, Carbone, did you forget how to salute?"

"No, sir."

Beasley's eyes widened. "Well?"

Sal bit his lip and squeezed the right handle tightly. His fake right arm jumped up to about chest height before dropping back down to his side.

"Are you trying to be funny with that salute?" Beasley snapped.

"No, sir," Sal replied. "My arm is just a little stiff this morning."

"That's more than a little stiff," Beasley remarked. "Let me give you a scratch so I can get out of here."

There was a very uncomfortable moment of silence that was shattered when Beasley repeated his order at a higher volume. "Give me your memo book!"

The sweat was now pouring down Sal's face. "Would you mind reaching into my pocket and getting my memo book yourself?" Sal whimpered.

"Did you just say what I think you said," Beasley snarled.

Sal stammered and mumbled a few unintelligible words as he unsuccessfully tried to come up with some semi-reasonable explanation for his actions.

While Beasley waited impatiently for an explanation, another passenger entered the train. The short, slightly built man with the receding hairline was neatly dressed as he quietly moved toward an empty seat at the rear of the car. Lt. Beasley was staring daggers at Sal as the small man sidestepped around Beasley towards the empty seat. In an instant Sal was no longer focused on the daggers emanating from Beasley's eyes. Priority had shifted to the wild eyes of the small man and the real dagger he was wielding as he lunged toward Sal.

"Die, you fucking pig!" the man screamed as he plunged the knife into the chest of Sal's rubberized torso.

The assailant's scream was joined by many others as passengers scrambled to exit the car. One elderly woman fainted while another woman curled up in a fetal position in her seat and prayed. Lt. Beasley was knocked aside by the man's lunge causing him to perform something of an off-balance pirouette before falling into the empty seat. Beasley was convinced he had suffered some serious head injury because when he looked up he saw the knife sticking out of Sal's chest, yet Sal was still struggling to control his attacker. What made Beasley believe he was hallucinating was the fact that it appeared that Sal was using four arms in his battle with the perpetrator.

Thirty seconds later there was an eerie silence inside the car. Beasley was still slumped in the seat when he felt a hand on his shoulder. "Are you okay, Lieutenant?" Sal asked.

Beasley tried to quickly assess the scene. Sal Carbone was standing above him with no knife sticking out of his chest and no blood on his uniform shirt. The small man was lying face down on the floor of the car with his hands cuffed behind his back. Beasley made one other observation that confirmed the probability he had received a concussion, at minimum. Lying next to the perpetrator was a police officer with a knife sticking out of his chest – a headless police officer. Lt. Beasley's eyes rolled back in his head as everything went black.

When Beasley came to and began ranting about a knife sticking in the chest of a headless police officer, the emergency room doctor was about to send him to the psychiatric ward for evaluation. As much as he didn't want to, Sal knew he had to fess up to his scheme. Even though Sal had disarmed a knife wielding assailant, he received no commendation for his actions. And although his admission saved Lt. Beasley a trip to the psycho ward, the Lieutenant expressed his gratitude by writing Sal up for violating the department manual rule against sitting while on patrol.

...

Doug Collins shook his head. This incident binder was a treasure trove of information that was perfect for the unit citation request. His fingers were working the typewriter at a pace he didn't think he was capable of. He couldn't wait to continue going through the binder.

CHAPTER 10: The Story of Police Officer Paul Kennedy

During the 1960s, Ed Sullivan would regularly have a plate spinner on his very popular variety show. The plate spinner was a man who would come out on stage to the rhythm of fast temp music and begin spinning plates on top of long sticks. He would keep adding plates until he had as many as eight or more plates spinning at the same time.

Paul Kennedy was a plate-spinner in a symbolic sense. In the policing profession it was very common for cops to establish "second fronts," or jobs that they performed during their off-duty hours to make extra money. Off duty employment was so common that there was a section of the department manual that spelled out regulations and restrictions to off-duty employment. Like many cops, Paul Kennedy had a second front. The nineteen-year veteran was assigned to the Train to the Plane Unit working 8 a.m. to 4 p.m. with weekends off. Paul was mechanically inclined, and several years earlier he had purchased an old, run down limousine which he proceeded to slowly restore until it looked good and ran efficiently. The limo became Paul's second front. On weekends he provided limo service to weddings, parties, trips to Atlantic City, and anywhere else a customer wanted to go in a limo.

Paul made a decent second income with his limo business and he followed all the department regulations regarding off duty employment. It wasn't his limo that made Paul a plate-spinner. Just as the performer on the Ed Sullivan show always tried to get one more plate spinning regardless of how many he already had up, Paul was always looking for another way to make money, no matter how many other jobs he was juggling. At his best Paul was working on a per diem basis at his friend's auto repair shop, working an adult paper route, picking up money at hospitals for a TV rental company, and working security at a topless bar. Paul was always scanning the horizon for other jobs to fit around his police schedule, especially when two of his plates tumbled to the floor. The topless bar was closed by the State Liquor Authority, and the TV rental company changed the route to include a hospital two hundred and fifty miles away, with the only additional compensation being the additional gas mileage.

It was one of the regulars on the Train to the Plane that provided Paul with the inspiration for another plate. Amy Carmona was a flight attendant for Delta Airlines. The petite, attractive 45-year old was one of Delta's senior flight attendants, having spent 23-years with the airline. Amy lived with her husband and three children in Miami, and for the past three years she worked a Miami to JFK route. She didn't particularly like New York, but the schedule worked well for her. She worked an afternoon flight from Miami to JFK and spent the night in a Manhattan hotel before flying back to Miami on a flight the next morning. What made this job attractive was that even though she was away from home for the night, she was off for two days after her return flight. On her return flight day, Amy was one of the regulars who Paul regularly conversed with during the trip to Howard beach.

The ride began in the usual fashion with the Train to the Plane slowly gliding out of 57th Street. Amy had been one of the last passengers to board the train, so she was still arranging her luggage in the overhead rack when the train entered the blackness of the tunnel. Amy finally settled in her seat and took a deep breath. She turned toward the rear of the car, smiled and waved.

Paul smiled and walked over to the flight attendant. "Good morning, Amy."

"Morning, Paul," she smiled.

"How are you today?" Paul asked.

Amy shook her head. "As usual, I'm running late. I just made it to the train and no offense, but these luggage racks are horrible."

Paul laughed. "No offense taken."

"And the luggage racks on that shuttle bus are worse," Amy continued.

"What are you gonna do?" Paul shrugged.

"They should have some type of car service as an option to that bus," Amy suggested. "I'll bet a lot of people would pay extra for a comfortable car ride to the airport instead of that cramped, uncomfortable bus – I know I would."

Paul stroked his chin. "That's interesting."

Amy continued talking about her husband's job and her son's baseball team, but Paul didn't hear a word. That light bulb that had just illuminated above his head required all his concentration.

Karen Kennedy had mixed feelings about her husband's industrious nature. On one hand she admired Paul's drive to go out and make money for the family, especially to give the kids things they wanted. On the other hand, however, the constant scheming new angles to make money had worn her down, especially when the schemes impacted her directly. Such was the case with the limo. Karen thought the vehicle was just something Paul had bought as a hobby to tinker with, but when he had completed his restoration project she was shocked when Paul announced that he had sold the family car. In Paul's world there was nothing wrong with using the limo as the family car. The kids were thrilled but Karen was mortified to be driving to the supermarket in a limousine.

Karen became aware of Paul's latest brainstorm when he began leaving for work much earlier than usual. The Kennedy's lived in the Nassau County Village of Floral Park, a three-minute walk from the Floral Park Long Island Railroad Station. For his 8 a.m. shift Paul would leave his house at 7 a.m. and jump on the 7:05 express train to Penn Station. He would arrive at Penn Station at 7:30, and jump on the subway, walking into District 1 at Columbus Circle at around 7:50.

When Paul began leaving the house at 5:45 Karen became suspicious. Was her husband involved in some early morning triste with another woman? When Karen confronted Paul and received the explanation, part of her wished there was another woman involved instead of the truth.

Paul explained that he had to leave early in order to drive the limo to Howard Beach. He would park the limo near the subway station and then take the train into Manhattan. The obvious question was why would Paul add over an hour to his commute by driving to Howard Beach. In Paul's mind, the answer was simple, and brilliant. He kept thinking about what Amy Carmona had said about the uncomfortable nature of the shuttle bus, and how people would pay extra for a comfortable ride to the airport. After Paul's second train run to Howard Beach he received his meal break. He usually bought a slice of pizza and sat in the porter's room until it was time for his train back to Manhattan. But why would he sit in a dark, dank porter's room when there was money to be made.

Two weeks before Paul sat at his kitchen table explaining the situation to his wife, he began carrying something extra with him on the Train to the Plane. He stashed them in the locked operator's cab and only broke them out at the start of his second train run. The brightly colored, professionally printed flyers read, *TIRED OF THE CRAMPED UNCOMFORTABLE BUS. TAKE A LUXURIOUS, COMFORTABLE LIMO TO THE AIRPORT – ONLY $10*

Paul could get six people comfortably into the limo. He considered stuffing more in, but he knew he would be shooting himself in the foot. After all, why would someone pay $10 to avoid a cramped, uncomfortable bus ride only to end up with a cramped, uncomfortable limo ride? Paul very proudly explained that he was selling out the six seats in the limo every day he worked. Instead of gobbling pizza in the porter's room he was using his meal time to take a quick ride to the airport and put $60 cash in his pocket. Paul said that after two weeks he had sold out the six seats every day, resulting in $300 extra a week.

Paul never had another $300 week. In fact, his gravy train derailed two days after the explanation to his wife. It seemed that riders on Paul's second train loved the limo idea, and many were disappointed when they could not secure one of the six available seats in the limo. The Transit Authority president's office began receiving letters praising the authority for providing limo service to the airport, and urging them to add additional limos so that everyone seeking the service could be accommodated. Some of the letters included copies of Paul's flyers. It took T.A. investigators one day to figure out who the limo driver was.

Lt. Beasley wrote a complaint charging Paul with a violation of department rules and regulations regarding the regulations for off duty employment. Paul pled not guilty to these department charges and demanded a formal departmental hearing. At the hearing, Paul attempted to use a very unique defense. He stated that he could not have violated off duty employment regulations because he was not off duty when he was driving the limo. Paul's defense theory did not sway the hearing officer. He was found guilty of all charges and given a ten-day suspension. That suspension ate up all of his meal time limo money and more. From that point forward, Paul went back to eating pizza in the porter's room. But he always was ready to spin that next plate at a moment's notice.

•••

Doug was satisfied that he had more than enough material for the unit citation request. There was still one more incident report in the binder, however, so to be thorough, he took a deep breath and commenced reading.

CHAPTER 11: The Story of Police Officer Jerry Combs

This incident was not odd, weird, or involved some elaborate scheme. In fact, it was very simple and straight to the point. Lt. Beasley had written up Police Officer Jerry Combs for being off post. For the Train to the Plane Unit, off post meant only one thing, Jerry violated Beasley's prime directive and had gotten off his assigned train.

It was during an early Sunday morning that Jerry Combs committed the unspeakable act of abandoning his train. When the train pulled into Broadway Nassau at around 8:30 a.m. and the doors opened, Jerry's conversation with an attractive flight attendant was interrupted by the screams of a female that seemed to be coming from the back end of the island platform. The platform was scarcely populated, but as Jerry stepped off the train several bystanders pointed towards the rear of the platform. One very animated man said, "Hurry, the guy is dragging the girl up the stairs!"

Jerry was off and running towards the rear of the platform. He flew up the last stairway and paused on the mezzanine. A few unconcerned riders walked past him. He didn't see or hear anything that remotely resembled a crime. Jerry continued ascending until he reached the street. Still, there was no victim or perpetrator of a crime. He reversed course back to the IND platform. All the pointers and the animated man were gone, and most distressing, the Train to the Plane was gone too.

The only thing Jerry could do was take the next A train to Howard Beach and catch up with his next Train to the Plane run before a sergeant found him off the train. Any hope of getting away with abandoning his ship was dashed twenty minutes later while Jerry still waited for an A train on the Broadway Nassau platform. The radio on a Sunday morning was usually very quiet, but suddenly the airwaves were bursting with activity. Police officers were frantically shouting over the air. Sergeants, lieutenants, and even a captain joined in. Jerry held the radio to his ear as he tried to figure out what was happening. When it became clear what had happened, Jerry had to rush to the nearest trash can to get sick. The Train to the Plane had been robbed at Jay Street, the first stop after Jerry detrained.

It seemed that when the doors opened at Jay Street, two masked men armed with handguns burst through the open door and robbed the conductor of his cashbox and all the passengers of their money and some jewelry. No one was injured in the robbery, and Jerry Combs, with his head dangling over the trash can, appeared to be the only person suffering any physical ailments as a result of the crime.

Naturally, Lt. Beasley was livid. If it was his decision he would have sentenced Jerry to life in prison without the chance of parole for having the audacity to get off the train. As it was, Beasley wrote Jerry up for any charge he could think of, including being off post, improper patrol, and insubordination. His department hearing and penalty was still pending.

Doug closed the binder, sat back and stretched. He still had a few final touches to put on the unit citation report, but he could not stop thinking about the great train robbery caper. He found something very curious about the circumstances. Doug was pretty sure he knew a way to satisfy his curiosity, but he would require help.

CHAPTER 12: The Band Gets Back Together

Doug met Police Officer Jenny Sanders when they both were assigned to the Delta Squad of the Decoy Unit. Delta Squad disbanded when its mission was complete but Doug and Jenny's relationship was still going strong.

"Hey babe," Doug gushed, "how's my favorite cop doing today?"

"I'll be doing a lot better if you take me out to dinner tonight," Jenny replied.

"Your wish is my command," Doug said.

"You're too easy," Jenny chuckled. "I feel like I need to do something for you now."

"Now that you mention it," Doug sang, "there is something."

"Oh boy," Jenny moaned, "here it comes."

"It's not a big thing, Jen. Is your friend Natalie Martinez still working at the Communications Unit?"

"She is," Jenny replied.

"I need you to arrange a favor with her."

"What favor?" Jenny asked.

"I'll explain over dinner." Doug said. "We'll go someplace new."

"Where?" Jenny asked.

"A place in Sunnyside," Doug said. "One of the cops here said they have a fantastic burger."

"What the name of the place?" Jenny asked.

"The Rising Moon – I think," Doug said. "It's on 44th Street off Queens Boulevard."

"What time?" Jenny asked.

"I'll see you at six," Doug said. "Love you babe."

At 6:10 p.m. Jenny turned off Queens Boulevard and picked up the pace of her walk on 44th Street. She slowed down as she caught sight of the sign. The Rising Moon was a small bandbox of a bar. The glass door was painted over and the windows had thick curtains in front of them. An Irish flag was hung in the window and a crude sign was put up letting the neighborhood know that this would be the headquarters of the Northern Ireland Aid Committee. Jenny placed her hand on the rough paintwork coating the door and pushed. Rough wooden splinters cut into her palm and shards of black paint crumbled to the floor. The hinges squealed as if offering a warning, but their plea was silenced by the noise inside the bar.

Laughter overpowered the jukebox. Conversations swirled in a dirty cloud of smoke. Two men with thick Irish brogues furiously smoked cigarettes and played a game of pool. Jenny was immediately annoyed when a scan of the bar revealed that Doug wasn't there yet. The bartender seemed nice enough when he smiled as he placed a gin and tonic in front of Jenny. She sipped her drink and watched the action in the small bar. Men walked in from their construction jobs with dusty jeans, boots, and big thirsts. They sat and laughed at the bar. Jenny tried to listen in but the juke box was loud, their voices were low, and their accents thick. Jenny continued to scan the bar while nursing her drink. On the poorly illuminated wall above the pool table she saw a Celtic cross dedicated to several IRA patriots.

Jenny's appreciation of the décor was interrupted by a kiss on the cheek. "Sorry I'm late," Doug said.

"That's okay," Jenny chuckled, "I was just about to join the IRA."

"Not so loud," Doug whispered. "I get the idea that they take that stuff seriously in here."

"Who the hell told you about this dive?" Jenny groaned.

"That's not important," Doug replied. "It's the burger that is the key, so let's move to a table and get to work."

The bartender was also the waiter, and after their burger orders were taken, Doug explained the favor he needed from the communications unit. "The CU keeps transcripts of all radio transmissions."

"So?" Jenny remarked.

"So, I want to get my hands on some of those transcripts without going through any official channels."

"What are you driving at?" Jenny asked.

"It's just a theory," Doug began. "What if that Train to the Plane robbery wasn't a random act by two mopes at Jay Street. What if the caper began with getting the cop off the train at Broadway Nassau."

"How would that work?" Jenny asked.

"What if the female screaming at Broadway Nassau was the ploy used to get him off the train."

Jenny shook her head. "I don't know about that. I read the report and there were several people on the platform who heard screams. Are you saying that all those people were in on it?"

"I read the report too," Doug shot back. "You're right, there were a bunch of witnesses to the screaming, but there was only one guy who claimed to see the female being dragged up the stairs. And the cop who jumped off the train could not locate the female or the witness who saw her being abducted."

"I'm still not following you, Doug."

Doug placed his hand on Jenny's forearm. "Suppose to wanted to hit the Train to the Plane. The first thing you would need to do was get the cop off the train, right?"

"I guess so," Jenny nodded.

"And what better time to get the cop off the train than at Broadway Nassau, the last stop in Manhattan. When the train gets robbed in Brooklyn, the mopes are hoping that no one is going to connect the cop getting off the train in a different borough with their caper."

"You may have something there, Sherlock," Jenny agreed, "but why do you need the radio transcripts."

"I want to check the radio traffic on Sunday's for the weeks leading up to the robbery."

Jenny smiled and nodded. "I think I see where you're going with this."

"That's right, babe," Doug said. "My asshole lieutenant has an edict in place that prohibits the cops from getting off the Train to the Plane under any circumstances. Most cops in the unit don't want to do any police work so they have no problem complying with the regulation. The others are too scared of the lieutenant's wrath to risk dumping their train."

"But that cop got off the train right before the robbery," Jenny commented.

"That's right," Doug said, "and personally, I believe he did the right thing, but the scumbag lieutenant wrote him up and charged him with everything short of the Kennedy assassination."

"So, you think the crew that pulled off this robbery may have tried to coax other cops off the train." Jenny said.

"That's why I need the radio transcripts," Doug nodded. "I want to see if on the Sunday mornings prior to the robbery, there were cops coming over the air reporting that they were getting reports of screams on the platform, particularly at Broadway Nassau."

"I'm off tomorrow," Jenny said, "I'll pay Natalie a visit in the CU tomorrow morning."

An Irish brogue cut into the conversation. "Here ya go, folks – enjoy" The waiter placed the two burgers on the table.

Doug took a firm grip of his burger in his right hand and extended it towards Jenny. "Cheers," he said.

"Oh, we're toasting with cheeseburgers," she chuckled as she tapped her burger to Doug's.

They both took big bites to complete the toast. As they chewed they stared at each other but neither said a word. Jenny was the first to swallow and provide commentary. "That was awful," she moaned.

Doug took a deep breath and bit his lip. "I wouldn't say it's awful," he said. "I would say horrendous is a much better description. Let's get out of here."

"I'm with you," Jenny replied.

Doug hesitated as he rose from his chair. "Oh, and please remind me to have a long talk with the cop who recommended this place."

The following morning Doug was feeling especially upbeat – so upbeat in fact that he decided to make himself at home sitting at Lt. Beasley's desk. He had run through his mind all morning how the scene would unfold when Beasley arrived, and the thought of it made him very happy. Beasley would immediately become annoyed when he walked in and saw Doug lounging behind his desk. Before the lieutenant could let out a blast, Doug was going to hit him with the completed unit citation report. Beasley would read the report and see that he was requesting that his unit be honored because members of his elite unit flew to Florida while on duty, took the place of the token clerk in the booth, sold soda and candy on the train, gave violin performances on the train, allowed a twin brother to impersonate him, defecated in a porter's room, and ran a limousine service while on duty. Doug was sure Lt. Beasley would erupt and they would have it out once and for all. Maybe he would transfer him on the spot. Doug didn't care. At this point any assignment would be better than the Train to the Plane.

The office door opened and Beasley stopped short when he saw Doug behind his desk. Doug followed his script by extending the report towards the lieutenant. "Here," he said. "this is the completed unit citation report."

Beasley snatched the report and also picked up a folder from his desk top. Doug was confused when Beasley did and about face and stepped towards the door. "Aren't you going to read the report?" he asked.

Beasley kept moving through the door. "Later, I have a meeting at Jay Street and I don't want to be late." His voice trailed off as he approached the exit to District 1, but Doug could still make out a final call. "And get out of my chair."

Doug was in no hurry to comply with Beasley's last order. In fact. He put his feet up on the desk and opened the newspaper. He had paged through the entire sports section when the desk phone buzzed.

"Collins," he answered.

Sergeant Will Henderson, the District 1 Desk officer was on the line. "Call for you on line 3, Dougie."

"Thanks, Will," Doug said as he pushed down the flashing red button.

"Collins."

"Hey babe, it's me." There was an air of excitement in Jenny's voice.

"What's up, Jen?"

"I'm at the CU with Natalie. She won't let me take any transcripts out of here but she let me review them here."

"And?" Doug asked.

"And you were right, babe. On the three Sunday mornings before the robbery there were radio calls from the cops on the Train to the Plane stating that members of the public were reporting hearing female screams at Broadway Nassau. And in each case the district and precinct responded but found nothing."

"I knew it," Doug declared.

"There's more," Jen broke in.

"What?"

"The same thing happened this past Sunday."

"So, they're trying to pull off the same caper again," Doug said.

"Why not?" Jenny said. "They got away scot free the last time. Why not double up."

"I think you're right," Doug said.

"What are you gonna do now?" Jenny asked.

"I'm gonna call an old friend."

...

"Hey Al, It's Doug."

The voice on the other end of the phone didn't seem overly enthusiastic. "To what do I owe the pleasure of this call," Lt. Al Harlan asked.

"Don't worry," Doug began, "I didn't call to break your balls about getting into the plainclothes task force anymore. I have come to the realization that I will be a Train to the Plane hairbag for the remainder of my career."

"And you called to advise me of that revelation?" Al chuckled.

"No," Doug replied, "I actually have some police work you might be interested in."

Doug explained his theory and what he had discovered from the radio transcripts. He finished up by adding, "If you're going to move on this, Al, I highly recommend that you say nothing to Beasley. The man could screw up a wet dream."

"I think you have something, Dougie," Al said. "I'll have a plainclothes team work it this Sunday."

"Who are you gonna use?" Doug asked.

"Your old squad is available this weekend," Al replied. "Gilligan, the McIntosh twins, and your girlfriend. Jenny is still your girlfriend, isn't she?"

"As far as I know she still is," Doug laughed.

"The only problem," Al continued, "is that Freddy Munoz is their team sergeant and he is on vacation. I wouldn't send them out on an operation like this without a sergeant." The phone was silent for a few seconds before Al continued. "It's gonna be hard to find a sergeant to come in on Sunday morning, even on overtime."

"I know a sergeant," Doug announced.

"Somehow, I knew you would," Al laughed.

"Will you clear it for me to do it?" Doug asked.

"Consider yourself cleared," Al replied.

"You can do that?" Doug questioned.

"Hey," Al said, "I'm part of the Citywide Taskforce and so are you. I can do what I want. Just work Sunday and I'll tell Beasley about it on Monday. He won't have a problem with it, and if he does I'll borrow Chief Reed's flyswatter and smack him."

...

At 5:30 a.m. on Sunday morning Doug walked into the District 1 muster room and smiled at the group assembled at the picnic-style table. "Seems like old times," he grinned.

There were four individuals sitting on both sides of the table. Jenny was joined by Gilligan, with the McIntosh twins leaving room for no one else on the opposite side.

Gil was named for Gilligan, his parent's favorite TV show. This was a nickname because his Korean-born parents wanted Gil to be Americanized and figured there wasn't very much American about his birth name – Dong-Suk Wang. When Gil was plucked out of the Police Academy to join the Decoy Unit to play the role of an Asian high school student, he was a small, slightly built, intelligent, quiet young man. Almost two years later he was still small, slightly built, and intelligent, but he was much more outgoing after being exposed to the world of the Transit Police.

The McIntosh twins weren't really twins nor were they brothers. Ron was Black and Don was white but they did share many similar traits. They were both over six feet tall, weighed over 250 pounds and were football players in high school. They also shared an aggressive attitude towards policing evidenced by the astronomical number of civilian complaints they had lodged against them. They had been snatched from patrol to provide muscle for the Delta Squad and now Doug was going to use their muscle again for his operation.

Doug briefed his team on the information he had and then got right into the tactical plan for the operation. "The Train to the Plane departs 57th Street at 8:05. That's our train."

"We're all gonna be on that train?" Ron asked.

Doug shook his head. "No, you and Don are going straight to Jay Street. I want you guys on that platform when the train pulls in."

"What about Gil and me?" Jenny asked.

"You and Gil are going direct to Broadway Nassau."

"Then what?" Gil asked.

"I am gonna be on the Train to the Plane." Doug said. "Once we get underway, I'll brief the cop on the train about the operation. When we're about to pull into Broadway Nassau, Jenny and Gil will be circulating around the platform and mezzanine areas ready to pounce on any screaming females."

"What about the cop assigned to the train?" Jenny asked.

"If we hear any screams or there are witnesses reporting screams I'm directing the cop to detrain and investigate."

"I get it," Gil said. "If Jenny or I see a female scream or someone telling the JFK cop that he saw a female being attacked, we follow the guy and grab him."

"You're on the right track, Gil," Doug said, "but not so fast."

"What do you mean," Gil asked.

"If this goes down the way I think it will, there's still one factor I'm not sure of."

"What factor?" Jenny asked.

"I don't know if the gunmen at Jay Street are making their decision to board the train after eyeballing it when it pulls into the station."

"What else would they be doing?" Don asked.

"They may be getting a call."

"Oh," Gil nodded, "you think that the crew at Broadway Nassau may make a phone call to Jay Street to let them know that the JFK cop got off the train."

"That's right," Doug replied. "And if they don't get that call, they may not hit the train."

"So," Jenny joined in, "if we do eyeball any part of the crew at Broadway Nassau we'll just keep them under observation until they make a phone call."

"That right," Doug said. "Any questions?" He clapped his hands. "Okay then, let's do this." He held up a red headband. "The color of the day is red."

Since it was Sunday morning an unmarked car was available for use by the team. The twins would drop Gil and Jenny off at Broadway Nassau before continuing to Jay Street. It was still very early so Doug declined a ride and instead took a slow stroll to the 57th Street station. He boarded the Train to the Plane at about 7:45 and displayed his shield to the conductor standing at the open door. There was no police officer in the car so Doug found a seat near the back of the car and got comfortable.

At 8:04 there were only eight other passengers on the train. Doug could hear the jingling of keys in the distance indicative of a police officer moving at a rapid pace. As soon as the uniformed officer was on board the two tones sounded and the doors closed. The conductor made the opening PA announcement and the train lurched forward. The cop began moving toward the rear of the car and stopped when he recognized Doug. "Hey sarge, what's up? Are you taking a flight this morning?"

"I wish, Kenny," Doug replied. Kenny Curran was in Doug's Police Academy class seventeen years earlier. Doug considered Kenny a very nice guy, but he wasn't too interested in doing any police work. Kenny was a consummate hairbag and a perfect fit for the Train to the Plane Unit.

"Don't tell me you're making a visit to beautiful Howard Beach," Kenny chuckled.

"Actually, Kenny, I'm working."

"Did you finally get into the plainclothes taskforce?"

"Just for today, Kenny," Doug replied, "and I need to tell you about what we're doing."

When Doug completed the briefing about the operation, a look of panic took over Kenny's face. "You want me to get off my train?" he gasped.

Doug nodded. "Yeah, if we get reports of a female screaming or being attacked at Broadway Nassau."

"But Beasley will skin me alive if I dump my train," Kenny groaned. "You know what he did to Combs, right?"

"Don't worry, Kenny," Doug assured. "I'm directing you to do this. I have your back and Lt. Harlan has my back."

"Well, if you're gonna take the heat, I guess it's alright."

When the Train to the Plane pulled out of Chambers Street, Doug raised the microphone of his radio to his lips as discreetly as possible. "Are you on the air, Jen?" The team was using a private radio channel so there was no need to use any codes.

"We're in place," Jenny replied.

"The train just pulled out of Chambers Street. We should be pulling into Broadway Nassau in about a minute. Do you have anything?"

"There's something interesting going on here," Jenny said.

"What is it?"

"There's a guy and a girl we saw together on the platform earlier. We saw them again a minute ago but now they've split up."

"Okay, keep your eye on them. We're pulling in now."

Jenny keyed her mic. "Gil, do you have eyes on either of our couple."

"10-4," Gil replied, "Curly is on the platform about fifty feet from me," he said, making reference to the man's long, curly hair. "He's standing near where the Train to the Plane's door will open."

Jenny could hear the rumbling of the train grow in intensity from her position on the mezzanine near the rear of the platform. "Okay, here we go," she said.

The train was a couple of seconds away from coming to a stop when a blood curdling scream rang out from the platform below where Jenny was standing. The person she had seen earlier with Curly, a young, pretty Hispanic female came up the stairs and paid Jenny no mind as she scurried along the mezzanine towards the front end of the platform.

The doors on the Train to the Plane opened and immediately Doug was blasted by cries from the platform. Doug could see at least two people frantically pointing towards the rear of the platform. A curly haired male was shouting about a female being dragged away by a man.

Kenny Curran suddenly seemed to have developed concrete shoes. He didn't move. Doug actually had to rise from his seat and kick him in the seat of his pants as discreetly as possible. With the additional motivation, Kenny detrained and was immediately engaged by Curly, who was waving his arms and pointing towards the rear of the platform. Doug watched Kenny disappear towards the rear of the platform. The two tones announced the closing doors and the train was in motion again. The next stop was Jay Street.

Doug pressed his mic to his ear so he could hear the transmissions from Broadway Nassau.

"Curly just went up to the mezzanine," Gil transmitted. "He just met up with a young Hispanic female."

"Stay on them, Gil," Jenny said, "I'm gonna find the JFK cop."

The train had to cross under the river and into Brooklyn, making it a six-minute trip to Jay Street. Approximately three minutes out of Jay Street Doug heard more traffic on his radio.

"They're in the street at the corner of Nassau and John Streets," Gil said. "Curly is using a pay phone."

"That's it," Doug transmitted. "As soon as he hangs up – grab them!"

"I'll be there with the JFK cop in thirty seconds," Jenny broadcast.

"Okay," Gil said, "he just hung up."

"We're coming up right behind you, Gil," Jenny announced.

Doug sat back in the seat and took a deep breath. The train was now less than a minute out of Jay street. Once again, Jenny's voice emanated from Doug's mic. "Two in custody at Nassau and John – situation under control."

Doug stood in the car, displayed his sergeant's shield, and addressed the twelve passengers and conductor in the car. "Would everyone please move to the rear of the car," he calmly stated. "There's a police action taking place at Jay Street so I just want to get everyone away from the doors."

There were a couple of questions being attempted, including from the conductor, but Doug shut them all down as the train roared into Jay Street. He took the seat directly across from the doors and placed his hand on the butt of the 2-inch revolver that was tucked inside a holster on his waist. He inhaled deeply and exhaled as the doors opened. The only activity visible were two men coming off the stairs from the mezzanine. These men could have been anyone rushing to make a train, but there was something different about these two. When they were about thirty feet from the doors Doug noticed that they both had something balled up in their hands. When they got to within ten feet of the door it became clear what they were carrying. The men were still moving forward as they reached up and pulled ski masks down over their faces. Doug unsnapped his holster and began drawing his gun, but he never cleared leather. It was as if the two masked men were swept away in a tornado, and in a way, they had been. The tornado that plowed into the armed robbers was named McIntosh. The twins had burst out of the porter's room where they had been secreted and executed perfect flying tackles. Before Doug could get out of the door the perpetrators were handcuffed face down on the platform with each smiling twin displaying a handgun that had been removed from each man.

"I didn't know you guys were capable of being so quiet," Doug laughed.

"We were in stealth mode," Ron smiled.

"Yeah, stealth mode and sack the scumbag mode," Don added.

...

The next morning there was much happiness within the Transit Police Department. All the top brass, including Chief Reed were thrilled with the arrest of the train robbers. Herby Dowdle was thankful for the good mood Reed was in. He may be free from browbeating and swatting for at least one day. Everyone at the Citywide Taskforce from Inspector Harrington on down were overjoyed that members of the Plainclothes Taskforce had made the arrests. Al Harlan was giddy on the phone when he called Doug to pronounce a job well done. The only unhappy person appeared to be Lt. Clifford Beasley. Even though a robbery of his Train to the Plane had been thwarted and the earlier robbery solved, Beasley was incensed that he had not been informed of the operation. What further frustrated him was that there was nothing he could do about his anger because the operation had turned out so well. All he could do was ignore Doug Collins.

Doug could empathize with Beasley's action because he usually did his best to ignore his lieutenant. In this case, however, he needed to interact with him once.

Doug stuck his head into the doorway of the lieutenant's office. "Could I talk to you for a moment?"

"What?" Beasley mumbled without looking up.

"You ran out of here quickly the other day with the unit citation report," Doug said.

"So?" Beasley replied.

Doug shrugged. "I just wanted to know if you had any comments about it."

Beasley sighed deeply and looked up for the first time. "To be honest, Sergeant, I didn't have the time to read it. I just signed it and forwarded it through channels."

"Really?" Doug remarked.

Beasley leaned forward in his chair. "I have faith that you wrote a good report. What's the matter, was there a problem with it?"

Doug waved both hands in front of him as he began to slide out of the doorway. "No problem, Lieutenant. No problem at all."

Doug walked into the muster room and saw Arnie Snell, a District 1 cop assigned to the roll call unit, sitting at the table eating his lunch. "Hey Arnie," Doug said, "do you know when they are going to announce the winner of the unit citation?"

"Next Tuesday," Arnie replied. "The ceremony is in the Chief of Patrol's office in Jay Street. Why, are you going?"

Doug smiled as he continued towards the locker room. "I wouldn't miss it for the world."

CHAPTER 13: Unit Citation

Herby Dowdle stepped behind the podium. "Would everyone please find their seats. We will be getting started momentarily."

The crowd in full dress uniforms that had previously been clustered in small conversation groups spread out throughout the conference room to take their seats. The commanding officers from all the districts and specialized units were present to see who would be recognized as the best command in the Transit Police Department with the announcement of the winner of the unit citation.

Al Harlan and Doug Collins were not representing any units, so they wore civilian attire and slipped into seats in the last row of the large room. Lt. Beasley did not acknowledge Doug and Al as he moved into a seat a row in front of them.

Al leaned forward and tapped Beasley on the shoulder. "Good luck, Cliff."

"Thanks," Beasley mumbled without turning around.

"He'll need it," Doug whispered.

"What's that mean?" Al asked.

Herby shouted, "Attention!"

The population in the room sprung to attention. Doug pointed to the door and nodded as Chief Reed entered the room. "You'll find out very soon."

George Reed placed a large folder on the podium and put on his glasses. "At ease," he grumbled. Everyone returned to their seats as the Chief looked out over his audience. "I've never been known for being an eloquent speaker, so I'll make this brief. It's a great honor to receive the unit citation and be recognized as the best command in the department and this decision was particularly difficult." Reed looked down and opened his folder. "A non-enforcement unit has never won the unit citation, and before I announce the winner I would like to ask Lt. Beasley to join me at the podium."

Beasley shot out of his chair with his chest puffed out as he hustled to the front of the room and stood next to the Chief.

"Lt. Beasley," Reed began, "as I just said, a non-enforcement unit has never won the unit citation." He took a deep breath. "And this year, your Train to the Plane Unit will not win the unit citation."

There was some low mumbling and snickering from the audience as Beasley's chest deflated and his eyes took on a glazed look.

"Even though your unit didn't win," Reed continued, "I wanted to recognize you and the Train to the Plane Unit for the wonderful report you submitted requesting the unit citation."

In the last row, Doug grabbed Al's forearm. "What's wrong?" Al asked.

"What's wrong is that I know what's coming and it aint gonna be pretty." Doug replied.

Chief Reed cleared his throat, "Lt. Beasley requested the unit citation for the Train to the Plane Unit by virtue of some amazing acts of some of the cops in his unit. First, there was an officer who flew to Florida while on duty. Then, there was a cop who gave violin concerts while on the train." Reed looked up to acknowledge a smattering of laughter. "Don't laugh too much," he urged, "you ain't heard nothing yet. Next there was cop who sent his twin brother in to work his shift for him, and another cop who sold soda and candy on the train. There was also a cop who rigged up a dummy on the train so he didn't have to stand." The Chief held up his hand to silence the howling audience. "Finally, there was an officer from the illustrious Train to the Plane Unit who was in the habit of taking dumps in a porter's room." Reed removed his glasses and turned to the weak-kneed Beasley. "No, Virginia, there is no Santa Claus, and no, Lieutenant you will not receive the unit citation. Frankly," he growled, "it is outrageous that you would submit such a report." Reed pointed to the back of the room. "Now, get back to your seat."

Doug noted that Beasley's face had transitioned from bright red to pale white as he slumped into the chair. Back at the podium, Chief Reed was ready to announce the winner. "Now that the clown show is over, I can get down to the business of the day. Like I said earlier, this was a very difficult decision, but something that happened last week tipped the scales. Members of the Plainclothes Taskforce made the outstanding arrest of perpetrators who were attempting to rob the Train to the Plane at gunpoint and who had, in fact, robbed the Train to the Plane two weeks earlier. Inspector Harrington, please come forward. It is with great pleasure that I award the unit citation to the Plainclothes Taskforce."

Applause filled the room as Harrington joined the Chief at the podium. The applause transitioned to a standing ovation from all but one in the audience. Lt. Beasley sat slumped forward with his face buried in his hands.

"Thanks very much, Chief," Harrington began. "It is a great honor to receive the unit citation and I accept this award on behalf of the hard-working men and women in the plainclothes taskforce."

More applause resonated.

"Thanks, Inspector," Reed said.

"Excuse me, Chief," Harrington cut in, "but there's one more thing I'd like to say."

"Go ahead."

"I would like to thank Sgt. Douglas Collins, who used his own initiative to conduct the operation that led to the arrest of the perpetrators from the Train to the Plane robbery."

Another standing ovation ensued. Even Beasley stood, but his motivation was to start easing his way towards the side door.

In the front of the room Chief Reed shook his head. "Alright Collins, I guess I have to put you back in the plainclothes taskforce."

Al Harlan slapped Doug on the back. Lt. Beasley gave a final look of disgust as he pushed on the exit door.

"Hey!" Reed bellowed from the front of the room, "Where do you think you're going?"

Beasley pointed to his own chest and squeaked, "Me?"

"That's right," Reed snarled. "Get in my office, now. I have business with you."

Beasley continued through the door while Reed scanned the room for Herby Dowdle. "Hey, you," he called out, "find my flyswatter. I'm gonna need it in a minute."

"No problem, Chief," Herby sang.

"Don't you feel a tad bit sorry for Beasley," Al asked as he and Doug exited the room.

Doug shook his head. "Not at all. And I'd love to be a fly on the wall in the Chief's office, even with a flyswatter being waved around."

About the Author

Robert L. Bryan is a law enforcement and security professional. He served twenty years with the New York City Transit Police and the New York City Police Department, retiring at the rank of Captain. Presently, Mr. Bryan is the Chief Security Officer for a New York State government agency. He has a B.S in criminal justice from St. John's University and an M.S. in security management from John Jay College of Criminal Justice. Additionally, Mr. Bryan is an Adjunct Professor in the Homeland Security Department and the Security Systems and Law Enforcement Technology Department for two New York Metropolitan area colleges